CAGED

A Jack Toback Novel

Book 1

Paul Falk

ISBN 9781794635319

Imprint: Independently published

Printed in the United States of America

CHAPTER 1

I've always been an avid history buff, when it comes to the United States penal system, specifically, California. It's where I've always called home, and I've no intention leaving anytime soon.

Technology has certainly changed over the centuries, but for all intents and purposes, the criminals have remained the same. The only thing though, they've gotten so much better at it. Incarceration provided all of the incentive and preparation that would be needed on the outside. Jail time wasn't intended to work that way. It's persisted that way for too long.

The population continues to increase at a dizzying rate and with it so does crime. It makes little sense to continue on the way we've been going turning out hardened criminals after their sentence had been served. We know no matter what we do, some can't be saved, but that does not speak to the majority of inmates. There's hope.

The single problem that has always plagued the prison system points to the fact that no steps have been implemented for any type of positive change. *Change*, that's the keyword. It seems like we keep waiting, for what I don't know. The other shoe had fallen a long time ago.

What is most needed would be to provide a program that would offer the inmates a genuine shot at rehabilitation. As it stands, there is no relationship between the California Penal System and Prison Reform, there never has been.

Sadly, there is no such thing as rehabilitation within the over-populated prison walls. Banging out license plates doesn't qualify. Nothing has changed since the first prison was first built thousands of years ago. We keep going down the same failed road. It would be madness to expect anything different unless an adjustment is enacted somewhere. Bold steps require bold measures. Speaking from personal experience, it's been long overdue.

Right now, prisons are being built at an alarming rate; they're going up all around us like weeds. With all my many years spent as Warden, barring any significant change, I see no way around the dismal direction we're headed.

To further exacerbate the problem, all the prisons operating within the state of California are burdened with inmates that greatly exceed maximum capacity. The Golden State's not the only place. The same applies to many throughout America as well.

The present population within our nation's industrial cities has continued to skyrocket to epic proportions. Unprecedented levels of unemployment have added fuel to the ever-spreading fire. Put it all together we have a recipe for civil unrest - disaster.

History has shown that there seems to be a cycle that comes about every 50 years or so. Maybe this is just a way of things shaking themselves out. It's never been understood. When it spikes, we can always expect an increase in crime. It's grown highly predictable. It's felt by many that we're on the threshold of the next cycle swing. Woe is us.

All of this is nothing new. For countless centuries, prisons have been bursting at the seams. Business had always been good. Demonstrations that had at one time been peaceful turned horribly, violent. Today, blood continues to spill onto our nations' streets. It has become a frequent occurrence and consumes along with it, untold collateral damage.

Everyone's a victim. Many innocent bystanders had become unwitting casualties of these senseless uprisings. The only change to come out of all this is a higher death toll. Something needed to be done, but no one had the immediate answers right at their finger tips. We certainly didn't want to bring about another Ruby Ridge, Waco or Los Angeles fiasco.

The pot's been boiling over for a long time now. For example, one particular study showed that crime had hit at an all-time high at somewhere around the beginning of the 22nd century, about a hundred years ago. Since then, it's been easily surpassed many times over. According to historical documents, the year 2132 appeared to be a breaking point. It was the straw. That's when we thought that it couldn't get any worse. It did. It went from the frying pan into the fire. Our penal system could stand no more.

Building more and more prisons is not the answer. Presently, many inmates had been released long before their sentences had been served. A great many of them were soon found guilty of another crime and sent back to lockup, a never-ending cycle; it's mind boggling. Other criminal offenders, depending on the nature of their crime were sentenced to serve their time out on parole. Some were directed to perform hours of community service.

They received no prison time for their crimes. There was no threat that posed to stop them in their life of crime. In this unfortunate case, crime pays. There's no way I can stand up and call that justice.

The underlying truth is clearly shown, for the most part, time and time again, the absence of rehabilitation of inmates had been the single leading cause of the breakdown within the penal system. Yet, we've continued to go about our merry way with blinders on.

This was not a revelation to anyone intimately familiar with the prison system. We watched this go unchecked for many generations. Something had to be done. No change means exactly that, no change. It was time to finally step in and take action. It's been a long time coming. My only hope would be for my generation to be the first to enact change, for the first time allow something positive to emerge. Born for this day, I was more than ready to meet this challenge head-on.

CHAPTER 2

I've spent my entire life in the Golden State and have always been proud to call it home. I'd served as warden of a medium sized correctional facility in Northern California for 16 years. Just over four years before that I was a correctional officer. It's hard to believe that twenty years had flown by so fast.

It had been my destiny at birth to rightly assume this honored position. Some family traditions are steeped with the police. Others are teamed with the fire department. Generation after generation, mine was with prisons.

After finishing High School, I packed my bags and headed off to college. I couldn't wait to get started. Shortly after graduating with a Bachelor's in criminal justice, I signed up to join the show. It couldn't have happened soon enough. This was something I had been preparing for my whole life. There was never a question in my mind that I might do something different. To me, there was nothing else.

Ask anyone in the prison system and they'll tell you there's only one way to properly learn the ropes. To me it means coming up through the ranks. This meant starting off as a correctional officer. My first years within the penal system gave me valuable front-line experience I would not have gotten in a classroom. There's no better way to learn about the workings of a prison than to jump right in and get your feet wet. It provided me with all the necessary building blocks that enabled me to jump start my career. I always had my eye set on the finish line and knew where I was headed.

As a little boy I'd seen my father go through it. He began the same way I had by working his way up through the ranks. He was a great inspiration; he was my hero. I've missed him since he's been gone.

Working in prisons had been a family tradition for many generations. It went as far back as my great-great-great-great-great-grandfather who was born on an infamous day in American history, September 11, 2001. I think I've got the number of 'greats' correct.

Today that date is still honorably remembered as 9/11. It will live on forever, and I see no reason why it wouldn't. The events of that tragic day are taught in every high school across America. I remember it well. Our text was titled 'We Will Not Forget'.

History recorded it as the day that a group of armed terrorists hijacked commercial airplanes and flew them directly into two skyscrapers in New York City into what was known as the World Trade Center. They both became towering infernos and had come tumbling down. Almost three-thousand lives were lost. The Pentagon had also been targeted. It was the worst act of terrorism to ever occur on American soil. We can only hope something like that never happens again.

It might have been being born on this memorable day was what later spurred the first of my family to stand up, put on the uniform and become an integral part of the prison system. There's been a lot of water under the bridge. To think, that was almost two hundred years ago.

In the inaugural year of 2023, Andrew Toback became the first of our family to graduate with a Bachelor of Science degree in criminal justice from San Diego State University. After serving as a correctional officer for several years he took his first post as Warden of a prison located in central California. And so, the stage was set.

Though long before my time, I regret never having met the man who would start this time-honored tradition. According to all the treasured family documents that had been handed down to me, I learned he left quite an impact upon the penal system. It left me with big shoes to fill. I probably never would.

Skipping ahead, history had shown that The United States would have to endure about another 80 years before a major overhaul to the penal system was ready to be implemented. Even though it was long before my time it couldn't come fast enough.

Finally, earlier this year, 2212, our first prison would become operational that would be run solely by artificial intelligence (AI) robots most commonly referred to as Droids.

A special facility located in southern California was built just to house them. During its construction, it was a constant source of discussion amongst everyone within the penal system. It remained at the top of conversations. When reported in the media, it sounded like pure science fiction. In many ways it still does. It was difficult for most people to wrap their heads around a prison that would be run exclusively by Droids.

* * *

It was just another ordinary day at work like any other until I received a call from California Governor David Ryan. It took me by complete surprise. It's not the first time we've ever spoken during my time as Warden. After going through the usual pleasant formalities, he didn't waste any time in getting down to brass tacks. That'd always been his style, shooting straight from the hip.

"Jack, I need someone I can count on to run the new Droid facility in Southern California. Would that person, be you? You know, I'm counting on it."

Where'd that come from? I almost fell out of my chair and without further thought replied, "I'm shocked Mr. Governor that you would consider me for such a high-profile position." There was a short pause.

"You've come well recommended and that's good enough for me."

He then proceeded to go over the expected date of opening which everybody and his brother in the penal system already knew about. Rumor had quickly spread nationwide that this wasn't just any prison. Not by a long shot.

It could always be expected that with anything new came waves of uncertainty. There's always uneasiness when we step away from the tried and true and move out of the comfort zone. I suppose that applies to almost everything of any significance.

It was the one and only one that the public and the penal system had kept a keen eye on. By some it had been hailed as the prison to end all prisons. To others they weren't so sure. Some groups were dead set against it. It was a mixed bag of opinions.

Rather than trying to play it cool and say something like, "I'll give it some thought and get back to you," I blurted out, "You can count on me Mr. Governor." My stomach was on fire. It was something I didn't need to think about. I accepted the position right then and there.

"That's great Jack. I'll get the wheels turning up here on my end. I'll need you to be down there and operational in 60 days. Will that pose any problems?"

Without hesitation I responded, "No problem at all sir." In my mind, I was already gone.

He said, "That's great Jack. I'll be in touch." The call disconnected.

From there, all things prison began to escalate and started to snowball. Without wasting any time, I received a message about an hour later from the governor stating that he had already lined up someone as my replacement. I thought to myself that was fast. But I suppose when you're Governor you can make things happen in a heartbeat. I'm guessing he'd already anticipated my answer.

Ten minutes later my phone rang and I answered, "California Department of Corrections this is Warden Toback."

"Well hi Jack, it's been a while."

I'd know that voice anywhere. "How've you been Irene?" I had met her at some meetings and functions of the prison system over the years and remember her well. To say the least, she's quite an attractive woman and that's putting it mildly.

She replied, "Since the governor called, I've been in a tizzy. I'd been offered and accepted the position as your replacement. I've been pretty busy, in my mind anyway for this monumental step. I couldn't be more excited for your upcoming move that we've all been talking about like since forever."

I stated, "Thank you for saying that. I was completely blindsided when I accepted the position only earlier." I continued, "No one's more deserving than you Irene for this move up the ladder from assistant Warden to Warden. You have my heartfelt congratulations."

"Thank you, Jack, you're so sweet. You're the first person I've spoken to about this."

It was time to regroup, so I asked, "How long before you'll be ready to climb aboard?"

Jokingly she said, "I'll be leaving tonight," she chuckled. "Seriously though, you can expect me in 30 days. Mark your calendar. I've already figured that's how long it'll take me to wrap things up over here," after a pause she said, "You know something? I'm really looking forward to the change."

I said, "A change you'll certainly get, and what's more, I couldn't be leaving this facility in better hands or more capable ones. I'm looking forward to your arrival."

Excitedly she said, "Thanks Jack. I'll see you soon." The call ended.

CHAPTER 3

Initially, I wasn't aware that my new prestigious assignment came with a couple of perks. They were delivered in the form of housing and a company vehicle.

There'd be no added stress of having to run myself ragged in search of suitable housing while running against the clock. That would be one less hassle.

I learned that my digs would be a condo. Terrific, that's what I'm living in now. Maybe I'll always live in a condo. Things could be worse. It turned out my future residence was approximately the same size as the one I own now. Logistically, that means my stuff should fit in there perfectly with no problem, not that I'd be moving down anything of intrinsic value. That would certainly make the transition from point A to point B a lot easier.

Of course, I'd continue to make my monthly mortgage payments on my condo here in Stockton. There's no getting around that. I'm not about to rent it out. You never know what the future holds.

The one I'd be moving to was scot-free, utilities not included. I guess you can't have everything. In the end it was a wash.

I'd be turning in my present car that was leased. I'm glad I had the foresight at the time of leasing it with the option to return it at any time.

Things were gradually beginning to look up. This is going smoother than I had imagined, off to a great start.

Thirty days rolled around. I really can't say if it seemed fast or slow. As promised, Irene showed up right on schedule. If such a thing was possible, she looked even better than I remembered. After cheerful greetings and hugs I escorted her into my office, that is, her office. We sat down and I poured us a cup of coffee.

I started, "Just so you know, I'll be able to stay on for as long as a month. Somewhere around that time I'll need to leave for my new post. I'm hoping that will give you enough time."

She looked thoughtful. After a sip of coffee, she returned, "That's awfully considerate of you Jack, but I feel a couple of weeks would probably do me just fine."

I let that sink in. This woman obviously has a good head on her shoulders. "Of course, that's entirely up to you but we can play it by ear one day at a time."

I could see that she made her position clear. In two weeks, I'm out of here. I'd grown attached to this facility and the many people I rub elbows with.

Actually, I couldn't blame her. If I was in her position, I'd want to gain full control of the prison the sooner the better. She's been on the job for many years. She's no rookie. As assistant Warden at her last job, she already performed many of the functions that are required of the Warden.

Those two weeks passed quickly, in fact, too quickly. It didn't take long for me to discover that I liked being around her. All of a sudden, I was in no hurry to leave.

Irene showed grit and confidence in her new role as top dog. Everything I introduced her to she picked up naturally. It certainly made it easy for me. All of this was all right down her alley. It gave me a secure feeling of confidence that I was leaving my prison in capable hands. The last thing I wanted to do was leave somebody hanging high and dry.

With all of the close time we spent together we had come to know each other fairly well. But she probably knew me better than I knew her. I confided in her some parts from my past that I felt comfortable about sharing with her. I usually keep those things to myself. Somehow with her, it just felt right. As the days passed, I had come to learn more about her. For one thing, she's been a native of Stockton her whole life, a real hometown girl.

On a few occasions after work we went out for drinks. She was always fun to be with. It hadn't taken long when I found myself beginning to regret my career move. I imagined how nice it would be getting to know her better. Just my luck, so I thought. On my last day at the prison we said our goodbyes. My time was up. Our time was up. I left that facility for the last time. It was time to get rolling though some inner force was pulling at me to stay. It was hard not to listen to it.

I drove straight home and hadn't been there five minutes when my phone rang. Called ID showed it was Irene. Uh-oh, something might have gone wrong at the prison. Anxiously, the first words out of my mouth were, "Is everything alright?"

She said in a harried voice, "Jack, I'm going to need the number of the fire department right away! Where do you keep it?"

It only took me a couple of seconds to realize that she was putting me on. I responded, "Well better than that, I've got several buckets here. I'll fill them and I'll get myself right over there." We both started laughing.

She said, "Seeing as how your wife's out of town maybe we can sneak out and have a couple of drinks tonight." Irene's a real card. She knows I'm not married.

I smiled to myself and responded, "She also took the kids with her so we're good to go." That brought on a little more laughter.

After a short pause Irene asked, "How about if we meet at Sal's at 8 p.m.? Do you know the place?"

"Like the back of my hand," I said. "That's the nicest place in town. I didn't know you knew the area so well." I already knew she'd grown up here.

"That's what makes me so complicated," she retorted.

I chuckled. "Great, I'll meet you there," and ended the call.

Where did that come from? I mean, we've gone out before a few times for drinks after work but Sal's? Here I go again, end-to-end head talking. I do this all the time. Anyway, I still had a couple of hours to kill before we would rendezvous. That's not very long to keep myself occupied.

First thing I thought I'd do is check my minimalist wardrobe. I've never been a fashion plate. To start things off, I noticed my shoes could use a shine. Tonight, would not be a night for sandals. My father used to say, "You can't impress a woman by looking like a bum." I loved him but a poet he wasn't.

It took me a few minutes to find my beloved shoe shine kit. It had been stashed away in one of the many boxes I had packed for my move. Step number two, I spread out some newspaper on the floor, a cushion for my butt and got to work. When finished, I was pleased with the results. My father had trained me well. I could see the reflection of my face in them. I do good work if I do say so myself, I reflected proudly.

So now I can check that one small detail off the list. The shoes are ready to go. Okay, I thought what's next? Pants would be nice. I've got a nice pair of black pants still hanging in the closet. Black goes with anything, right? They appeared clean with no creases in them. They'll do.

Socks, I've got several pairs of black ones, somewhere. A search for them had turned up empty. It looks like black socks are out. I could feel a nervous sweat coming on. They must be packed away somewhere, probably at the bottom of one of the boxes, and I wasn't about to tear the place apart looking for them. I glanced at the time. It was not on my side. I've got brown ones. I guess brown's okay. Don't panic.

Then I thought to myself, Whoa Jack, what are you doing? You're just going out with a friend to dinner and a couple of drinks, nothing more than that. Try to get a hold of yourself. Casual attire will be just fine. Don't overdo it like you always do. I needed to reprimand myself. Nobody else would.

I didn't have to check my wardrobe for that. That's how I lived, casual. Even though I had already shaved this morning I thought I could use a slight touch up. Who am I trying to kid? I wanted to look my very best.

I finished everything off with another shower. I still had a little time left, though I didn't want to hurry and have everything come down to the last minute. I've always preferred to avoid rushing when at all possible.

After getting dressed I scrutinized myself in the mirror. Something didn't seem quite right. From the looks of it, I didn't look like someone who was going out on a date with a beautiful woman. I looked like I was dressed to go to the local supermarket.

That's not cool. I didn't look like any special catch of the evening. "Shit!" I said out loud. I can't go like this! This *is* a date. I'd better make myself look more presentable. What's the matter with me?

Now I was glad that I shined my shoes. At least that's one step in the right direction. My sports jacket had been recently pressed and hadn't been packed away yet. I was thankful for that. After another look at the time, I got out of my funky casual look and got dressed up. Standing before my full-length mirror I muttered, "Looking good Jack." Poised in front of the mirror, I looked like I was actually ready for a date, a real one.

I didn't move and remained in front of the mirror and stared at myself for a while and said out loud, "What the hell is wrong with you man?" I cupped myself on the side of the head and thought, this *isn't* a date. She's a friend. Although she's a friend I'm definitely interested in. I reminded myself that I'm leaving soon. So, I began to convince myself to see if just once I could just try to relax, for a change.

What happened next was comical. The only thing is that I was not laughing. I couldn't believe I was about to do this. For the second time, I got undressed and changed back into my casual outfit, if you'd call it that. If anyone witnessed what I'd been doing for the last hour they would have thought I was nuts. And by all accounts I'd have to agree with them.

I couldn't believe it, now I was running behind time. My sweat glands kicked into overdrive. I always prefer to arrive a little early when meeting someone. That's just how I've always been or used to be.   Now I'd be cutting it real close, too close. Charging out the door in haste I made sure that I had my wallet with me. With my car keys in hand I practically ran for the car.

On the way to the restaurant, with great restraint, I managed not to exceed the speed limit and arrived at the restaurant only a few minutes late. I'm rarely late for anything and of all times it had to be tonight! As I pulled into an empty spot in a packed lot I laughed and shook my head. What if she's all dressed up and I come walking in looking like a bum? Stupid... Stupid...

CHAPTER 4

I was too late. She had beaten me to it. Damn. I hurried from my car into the restaurant. When I identified myself at the check-in counter, I was told that a woman was waiting for me at a table. The hostess asked that I follow her to my awaiting companion.

It was now the moment of truth. In seconds I'd know how she dressed for the occasion. My palms were a bit sweaty. We rounded a corner and I saw dead straight ahead there she was facing me sitting comfortably at a table for two. Immediately, relief swept over me. I could see that she was also dressed casually. Now the laugh was really on me, but I thought I'd keep that to myself.

Playing Mr. Cool, I nonchalantly strolled up to where she was sitting and gave her a little peck on the cheek. She smelled fantastic. We smiled at each other and I carelessly, stumbled my way over to my seat. I'll bet she thought that was amusing. I told her that something minor had come up which forced a slight delay. I wasn't about to reveal how much of an idiot I had been.

She took a sip of wine and said, "That's quite okay. I've only been here a few minutes."

I could see that the restaurant was almost at full capacity. Must be doing something right, they always did a good business here.

Irene placed her wine glass down. "I forgot to tell you to dress casually," she said, "I'm glad to see that you did."

It was everything I could do to keep myself from bursting out laughing.

When I looked at her, I could see that she was staring at me and declared, "What are you all smiles about?"

I held my tongue. I didn't realize that I had been that obvious. I'd forgotten she was expertly trained in facial recognition, and beside the point, she's was a woman.

"Oh, nothing really," I offered hoping she'd buy that. Wonderful aromas swept along our table as other orders were taken to other customers. My appetite escalated.

After a quick perusal of the menu, we placed our orders. She opted for the chef salad and chose a glass of white wine to go with it. I decided on lasagna and a craft beer. It's my favorite go-with-anything beverage. No home cooking for me tonight. Actually, it was just plain nice getting out for a change especially, within the company of an intelligent, not to mention gorgeous woman.

Our dinners arrived about twenty minutes later. I've had their lasagna before. It's out of this world. I couldn't wait to dig in.

Initially, our conversation centered on work. In no time our plates were cleaned. We must have both been starved.

Changing topics, Irene smiled and asked, "What brought you into the prison system?"

After considering the question, I exclaimed, "That's going to call for another beer. How's your wine doing?"

"I'm still good."

I got the waiter's attention and ordered another drink. Looking back at Irene, I began, "I might as well start from the beginning. Way back when, I was born in a small town in East County, San Diego known as La Mesa. When I was just a toddler my dad started work at a prison not far from there as a correctional officer. Luckily for me I had a stay-at-home mom. I was an only child."

I cleared my throat, "Yeah, I know, you're probably thinking that I must have been a spoiled brat. You're right. When I was three years old my parents brought home a boxer puppy. I named her Tank. She'd be my new best friend."

I took a pull of my beer. "On many weekends my family would pack up our stuff and go out to a lake for a day of fishing. I remember that we usually fished off the dock. At places like that, Mom was in charge of food and settled her picnic basket on one of the park's many tables. Tank had the responsibility of running back and forth between the three of us. Those were the best of times." It all came rushing back to me. For a brief moment I lowered my eyes and stared at my hands.

As I finished the last of my beer, this time it was the waiter who signaled to me that he'd get me a refill. I nodded my acceptance. When I looked to Irene, I noticed that she dabbed at her eyes. I didn't ask why, perhaps I should've.

I could see that she was waiting for me to continue. After a moment, I said, "About the time I turned five my dad accepted a promotion that he had long been waiting for. He would be assistant warden in a Los Angeles jail. It was definitely too far of a commute. His career was calling, and so it was time to move."

Just then my drink arrived, saved by the beer. It was good timing. I took a healthy swallow while I gathered my thoughts. Irene stared at me and nodded indicating for me to go on. It was nice knowing that someone wanted to hear my life story other than the wall.

After a lengthy pause I began, "I started school there. My dad spent more time at work there than he did in San Diego. He told us there was a lot more responsibility that went with the new position. We all missed our time together. I probably asked him way too many times when we'd be able to go fishing. He usually said something like we'll go the first chance we get. When you're five years old missing a weekend seems like forever."

I took another pull from my beer and said, "Irene, I seem to be doing all the talking here. I don't want to monopolize the conversation. I don't want you to think that I'm a blabbermouth."

"It's okay Jack. Please go on. I want to know more about what makes you tick."

I enjoyed hearing that. "Where was I? Never mind, I got it. I was just finishing the eighth grade when it was time to move again. This time my dad won first prize and was offered the position he'd waited for over his entire career – Warden. This next relocation brought us up north to a prison not very far from here. It was something he had dreamt about."

My mom and I were happy for him. Tank didn't care one way or the other. Also, I was happy to be leaving Los Angeles behind.

"Do you remember how old were you at the time when you moved up here?" Irene asked.

"I'd guess I was somewhere around thirteen. That was when we moved into our first house right here in Stockton. It came complete with a fenced front and back yard that Tank would take full advantage of. I have fond memories attached to that house. I finished high school here. On some weekends we'd take trips out to Camanche Reservoir."

Irene said, "I know the place well. I've been there several times."

"We still had all the fishing gear we had in San Diego. It was like we never stopped. It came as second nature to us. There were times that on our way to the lake, we picked up some food to go."

I took another swallow. "We'd rent a boat and the three of us, make that four would be out on the water.

To add to the enjoyment, Tank would occasionally jump from the boat into the water in pursuit of a duck. That was hilarious. She never caught one but was entertaining to watch. When she realized the hunt was over, she made a beeline for the boat. We all laughed till our sides hurt with the time we had getting her bulk back on board."

I took a final swig of beer. "Mom usually packed beer, soda and iced tea. She wasn't much of a drinker and was the designated driver to bring us all home. It seemed that every problem in the world disappeared when we went out on these family get-togethers. I wanted it to last forever."

I signaled our waiter over. Before I could say anything, he asked, "Can I get you another round?" It must have been written on my forehead - beer here.

I answered, "Yes please."

Irene chimed in, "I'll have another one as well please." She nodded at me to continue.

I went on to say, "Let's see...Oh yeah, after High School I was admitted to CSU, Long Beach to begin my studies for a degree in Criminal Justice. The major was a no-brainer. It had been assigned to me at birth. I missed being away from home and came back every chance I got. During my first semester there, Tank died. She was a great loss to our family." I felt my eyes begin to well.

The drinks arrived just in time. We raised our glasses and clinked. I was lost in thought for a while. Irene remained silent.

"During my senior year at CSU, my mom was diagnosed with breast cancer. A biopsy showed that it was malignant. All I wanted to do was just drop everything and go home. Dad convinced me to hang in there. He kept saying that everything would be fine. He said that she's getting all of the best medical treatments that are offered."

I took another swallow. My stomach was getting tight. "I finished my last semester and returned home without delay. I'll admit it was difficult. When I got there, I'd seen that mom had lost a lot of weight."

She smiled saying, "No diet had ever worked this well for me before."

I couldn't find the humor in that remark and said nothing.

I stopped and had a long pull of my beer. When I looked up, I noticed Irene was wiping at tears that had run down her cheeks. I thought I'm one hell of a date. Now I've got her crying.

I said, "I'm sorry for..."

"Stop," she said. "You have nothing to be sorry about. We'll finish this conversation another time."

I added, "And there *will* be another time."

Dabbing at her eyes, she replied, "You can bank on it buster."

Other than my depressing life story, it was a fun-filled night out on the town. When the check arrived, I reached over to grab it but she snatched it up with cat-like reflexes. She whispered loud enough for me to hear, "Tonight's on me."

I said, "That's awfully generous of you but you shouldn't have, really." Did I just make that dopey comment?

She quickly looked over the bill and handed the waiter her card. It was too bad this all had to end so soon. I was beginning to feel an attraction to her like I've never had before. From what I've learned of her, she seems like a down-to-earth warm and caring person that I'd really enjoy getting to know more about. The way it looks right now, spending any more time together just wasn't in the cards, at least not now anyway. After all, I'm getting ready to take off for my new position in Southern California. I should blame this all on the governor. I need a fall guy.

When she settled the bill, we both stood and made our way toward the restaurant's exit. When we got outside Irene took my hand and we walked side-by-side. Upon seeing her to her car, she turned and said to me, "I'll see you in fifteen minutes."

For a moment I was dumbfounded. Somewhat speechless I could only come up with, "What are you talking about?" I could only imagine what a loser I must have sounded like.

She produced a devilish smile and said, "Remember when I said tonight's on me? Well the night isn't over yet big boy."

We laughed.

"Do you know where I live?" I asked.

"I'm way ahead of you. I've already scoped your place out."

I'll take that as a compliment," I said.

She barked, "You better."

She followed me home. I didn't know if it was unusually warm in my car or maybe it was me. Who am I trying to fool? It was me. I felt like a dog in heat. When we got there, she parked right next to me in a visitor's spot directly in front of my condo. When she got out of the car, I could see there was something in her right hand; it was a bottle of wine. She's just what I need, a woman who plans ahead. It looked like it was going to be party time. As it turned out it was a night I'll never forget. I hoped the same for her.

Sometime in the early morning I heard the bed rustle. I raised one eyelid and saw that Irene was already up finishing getting dressed. I whispered, "Good morning."

"Good morning Jackie." she replied seductively.

With a smirk I replied, "There was only one person in my life who ever called me by that name, my dad."

"So, now that makes two."

I could see that Irene was preparing to leave. "Can I at least offer you a cup of coffee first? It'll only take a few minutes. I have a state-of-the-art coffee maker," I pleaded.

"Thanks sweetie but some of us have to work for a living," she chortled. After slipping on her shoes she padded over to the bed, bent over and gave me one long smooth enticing kiss. She whispered, "That's going to have to last you until I see you next time."

"There'll definitely be a next time," I said. She smiled, turned and headed out through the bedroom door. I yelled out, "Don't forget, I know where you work."

There was no response to that. Ten seconds later I heard the front door of the condo close. I was sorry to see her leave.

CHAPTER 5

I'd never been married not that I have anything against that sacred institution. As far as appearances are concerned, I don't consider myself to be a bad looking guy, though I claim to be no door prize. I suppose the right one just never came along.

Maybe subconsciously, I've always placed the bar too high. I suppose that could have also been said of the women I've known, and there's been a few, a few too many. Being totally honest, perhaps they're the ones that placed it too low.

Given my present circumstances with relocating to Southern California and such, there's something to be said for being single, one of which is being able to move on a moment's notice. I had a handful of sour grapes reserved just for this very occasion.

The following morning, I watched a moving van pull away with my life. There's not a whole lot to it. Most of it was hand-me-down furniture which still only gave my condo the Spartan look.

Shortly after it got out of sight, I jumped into my new company car and took off for my new digs, new job and new life in Pasadena. I couldn't help but feel a bit adventurous. I hadn't felt this footloose and fancy-free since my old college days. Little did I know what was really awaiting me there? At least I had a place to go to and hang my hat. Wait, I don't wear hats. I'd have to put my heartfelt feelings for Irene on hold for a while. Secretly, I hoped it wouldn't be for too long. I was beginning to miss her already.

Never exceeding the speed limit, I made the drive to Pasadena in somewhere in the neighborhood of around eight hours. That took in a late lunch and a rest stop along the way. All in all, it was a smooth trip.

When I got to Pasadena my new place was easy to find. The car's built-in navigation system did all of the hunting for me. All I had to do was stay awake and turn the steering wheel. Even a monkey could do that. I was pleased to discover that it was a ground-floor unit. Perfect, that's what I have up in Stockton. It's exactly what I would have chosen. A quick scrutiny of the rooms showed that it was slightly larger than mine, a definite plus. I'll have a little more elbow room not that I really needed it. All that's missing now is my furniture.

Surprisingly, the moving van pulled in front of my unit shortly after I arrived, talk about timing… I'm not one who believes in signs, but if I was, I'd say that was a good one.

As my furniture was unloaded and carried in, I orchestrated where each piece was to go. There was a place for everything. In a little over an hour they were done and on their way. My minimalist lifestyle saw to that.

All that remained was unpacking a pyramid of boxes that were stacked six feet high. I'm glad I thought to have them labeled, this way it wouldn't be eenie meenie miney moe. I don't do this moving thing very often. Where's somebody to give you a pat on the back when you deserve one?

As far as I was concerned there'd be no rush in getting to them. If nothing else, my bed was set up and the two boxes labeled blankets/sheets, pillows/pillow cases and towels were right next to it. What more could I ask for? I could think of a few things.

I spent the first couple of days feeling my way around town. Pasadena's a charming place. It doesn't feel anything like the slower pace of Stockton. I'd only just arrived and already I was feeling a little homesick. I'd visited here before but that was quite a while ago. Some of my college buddies and I came down here on one of the spring breaks from school. That was back in my wild and crazy days so I'd like to think.

All of the major shopping attractions I had gotten used to back home were nestled in this quaint town. There was nothing missing, nothing other than Sal's of course. Shopping for food was within walking distance depending of course on how prepared I was to lug it all back home. I think I'll leave that type of exercise for the gym. They'll be plenty of time for that too.

First on the agenda was stocking my new home with food and beverages. There's nothing in this world more saddening than peering into an empty refrigerator.

I returned to my condo with three bags packed to the top with many contributions for the fridge. It didn't look like I'd be going hungry anytime soon. With my single most important domestic chore done, it felt like it was as good a time as any to check out the prison. From what I could see on the map, I'd guess it was no more than five miles away, tops. It would be an easy commute.

The drive transitioned quickly from city, to suburban and to rural like fanning pages in a book. Nothing about the lighting, street, or guardrails suggested anything even remotely related to country. Everything appeared of new modern construction and appeared meticulously maintained. It was evidence of our hard-earned tax dollars at work, some of it anyway.

As I wheeled up closer, my first glance at the prison left quite a lasting impression. There were no visible guard towers. Every prison had them. I'll have to take that back. Most have them. I remembered that we're in the Modern Age now. Had it not been for the sign as I approached that read Droid 1, I might have taken the wrong turn off.

After parking my vehicle in my own assigned spot which only took a few minutes to find, I guided myself through an elaborate maze of doorways and scanners that had been coded to the iris of my eyes. How they had gotten that information from me and had it installed I'll never know. I'll put that question on the back burner just for now. I finally made passageway into the belly of the facility. It was beyond what I had imagined. This was the most high-tech operation I've ever seen. It looked like mission control.

I hadn't been there very long when I received a memo from the governor's office on my phone. It was short and right to the point. A meet and greet with the governor, state assemblymen and the Press was scheduled for tomorrow morning. My presence was expected. It would have been nice if I had been given a little more notice. I'm certainly glad I hadn't made any pressing plans for tomorrow but then again when the boss speaks...

In the meantime, I'd familiarize myself with all the bells and whistles in this huge room of sophisticated electronics that was trying to pass itself off as my office. I remember seeing my name on a door, somewhere. If nothing else I'll try not to accidentally break anything.

I stood there and gawked. The surroundings gave the impression of something taken straight out of Science Fiction. It was a bit overwhelming, and for a fleeting moment I began to question myself if I was just a little bit in over my head. I wrote it off as first-time jitters. Besides, it was a little too late to even think about backing out now.

I had seen enough for today and decided it was time to head on back home. First stop along the way would be to pick up some cold ones. I don't know how I could have forgotten that when I went shopping. Note to self, next time make a list. Everything else was stocked to the till. I had no idea what to expect the next morning. Ignorance is bliss. So, I'll follow my gut instincts as I usually do and play it by ear.

Next morning when I arrived, I was overwhelmed by reporters and camera crews. Apparently, I was the first one not connected with the media to show up. The crowd gave all the appearance of a shark feeding frenzy. I tried to look confident and in control but who was I trying to kid? My nerves were on edge.

My phone trilled. It was the governor. This is one of the first times I was actually thankful to hear his voice. He asked me to bring everyone inside to the main hall as his limousine was pulling up. That drew the media to him like a magnet. Surrounded by the Press he was in his element. Time could always be allowed for a little publicity.

This was when I got my first look at the Department of Corrections droids. There must have been a hundred of them. It was only a drop in the bucket for what would eventually be required. I was actually amazed at how lifelike they looked. All were appropriately dressed in prison uniforms. They looked exactly like inmates. Had I not known better, I might have thought they were inmates preparing to start a riot. Naturally, they needed to blend in. I enjoyed a good laugh at myself. Did I expect them to be dressed in tuxedos?

As far as I knew, the first inmates weren't scheduled to arrive for another week. That would provide plenty of time to work out any kinks. Better to find any problems now even of the slightest than later.

The governor came over and pulled me aside and said, "They'll be coming in in droves. I expect to have this facility working at full capacity in 6 months." He nodded with confidence.

"That's great Mr. Governor," I responded. I thought that's awfully optimistic. But then again, I guess he can afford to be; he's governor.

At first glance I noted that all of the droids did not look exactly the same, skin color differed as well as hair length. I'd guess that height and build were all about the same - medium. Of course, they all looked male. Not one of them spoke.

When the questions, hand shaking and picture taking had finally subsided the media circus left the building. A small group of us gathered around a table and sat down. The group consisted of the Governor, Lieutenant Governor, three State assemblymen and three of the droids. The governor first addressed the droids and asked if any of them would like to make a comment. Without hesitation the one sitting directly across from me spoke up.

He introduced himself as Charlie. I was expecting to hear a number. But of course, a name sounds more personal. He carried our small intimate conversation for the next fifteen minutes. There wasn't anything in the world he couldn't expound about. Clearly, he was quite articulate in his manner of speech. It left me duly impressed and I looked forward to working with him - it.

Upon the conclusion of our not-so-casual meeting, the five dignitaries excused themselves from the facility. I assumed cocktails somewhere not too far off must be waiting. That left me alone with the droids.

One of the first things I had come to learn from Charlie was that unlike other prisons, the inmates would not rotate into cooking duties. That would all be accomplished by the droids. Each of the droids would transport the prepared meals from the cafeteria back to their cell. Then return the trays back again when finished.

Lesson number one: there'd be no commingling of prisoners in the main cafeteria. This was going to be a first in the history of prison reform. It was always at the cafeteria where many problems had arisen such as gang violence and drug distribution. There was no stopping it, until now.

The second area of concern in need of correction, and perhaps the most problematic within the penal system occurred during the one hour of exercise in the yard. This was the appointed time when the general population would all come together. For many it was an hour of gang meetings, drug deals and fights. Anything that could possibly go wrong was sure to find its way there.

Here at Droid 1, the required period of exercise would be conducted in an area outside that served each individual cellmate. It was constructed on artificial turf and was enclosed with solid walls, not fencing. In the event of rain an electronic sliding roof would cover the area. There'd be no inmate to inmate interactions at any time whatsoever. That took care of problem number two.

Charlie told me in brief terms that everything about the prisoner would be stored in the droid's memory: family, friends, wives, lovers, sexual preferences, history of employment, schools attended, arrest record, all known addresses, drinking/drug use, medical history and psychological profiles. He said there's much more but that would probably be enough for me to digest for now. He was right.

CHAPTER 6

The droids are a powerhouse of knowledge and would know more about the inmates than the inmates would probably know about themselves. They would use this information to find common ground with them. Their mission was to get through to each and every one of them in their own custom-tailored way.

The means by which this informal counseling would take place would be without the inmate's prior consent or knowledge. On the surface, it was intended to appear natural.

The proposed goal for introducing droids into the prison was to release back into society model citizens that the penal system, the state of California and the United States would be proud of. It sounded great to me and I was one-hundred percent behind it. If it offered any improvement to what we see going on right now, it's already a winner in my book. Let's get the show on the road.

This was the first and only prison of its type and was appropriately named Droid 1. Not much thought went into that one. There'd be no correctional officers at all except for the post of Warden. That would be me. I'd be the only one there with a pulse.

Far from being one of the larger prisons, its design and inmate population was intended mainly as the testing grounds of future prison reform. If proven successful which many felt confident about, it would act as the springboard to other prisons of its kind. It was an honor to be at the helm.

From the time of first breaking ground to the ribbon-cutting ceremony, the facility turned out to be a masterpiece of technology that would ultimately house 4,000 inmates. That would be a healthy start. Each cell is designed to hold one inmate and one droid.

Charlie stated what I suspected to be with a hint of pride, "Gangs, violence and drugs will not take place in this facility at any time."

That statement in itself is something that could never before be imagined. With those criminal activities successfully removed, a true shot at rehabilitation would find its way on the road to success. I didn't know if everyone invested was being too naïve. It just seemed too good to be true. There'll be only one way to find out.

I asked Charlie if there were any concerns about being overtaken physically by one of the inmates. He said that when he had gone through the testing facility in Sacramento, he was told that he had at least the strength of an adult Silverback Gorilla, probably more. I thought to myself, maybe I'll get to see that lab up north someday, hopefully soon. From what he said, apparently, the chances of being subdued by an inmate would be nil.

Charlie's voice did not sound robotic or monotone in any way. It was like talking to another guy. "When everything has been enacted as planned, what we'll have before us will be an environment for positive change," he assured me. "Nothing could possibly go wrong."

I'll admit it was comforting hearing those words rolling off his humanoid lips. Now only time would tell when the first inmates come rolling in. It won't be long now.

I knew that many long-term savings would be passed along to the state in the form of salaries, pensions, vacations and medical leave that would otherwise be paid to correctional officers. That would all be eliminated. The savings would be phenomenal.

Not so apparent at first would be the good fortune absorbed by our country from the former inmates becoming a productive member of society, no longer a leach. Nobody's put a number on that yet. It's too early to tell.

I learned that much of the funding to set up this facility had come from the federal government. They would be keeping close tabs on the development and progress of this facility; there was a lot riding on it. If successful nothing could stop this program from going nationwide other than funding of course. I was a bit nervous with the weight of the nation resting heavily upon my shoulders, make that our shoulders.

* * *

During the latter part of the 21st Century, research and development into artificial intelligence had made leaps and bounds. The days of robots being propelled on wheels and shaky legs were a thing of the past.

The goal had been to produce a humanoid of super intelligence with arms and legs that would mimic that of its creator.

Research scientists in the field of artificial intelligence had been looking to create a droid similar to the character of Data from the famed hit TV show of the twentieth century, Star Trek. I've seen the show. Ideally, the more human looking the droid the better. It was a daunting task that took generations to be where it is today. Anything looking like a clod or clumsy oaf would not cut it.

When I got home, I received another memo from the governor's office. It read that I would be leaving tomorrow for a three-day period of training at the testing labs in Sacramento. It was what I had been hoping for. It seemed like the right thing to do, especially, before we began admitting inmates. I would be spending some valuable time at the science lab housed within the California Department of Prisons headquarters. That sounded exciting and I couldn't wait to get hands on experience. It would be just what I needed, I was sure of it.

Lately, the way things had been going, everything so far seemed to be scheduled for the next day. I was told that someone from the department would be picking me up at precisely 8 a.m. and taking me to Hollywood Burbank Airport, a relatively short hop from Pasadena. From there I would connect with a direct flight to Sacramento. Carry on luggage would suit my needs just fine. I'd only be there a few days.

I would be staying at the Hampton Inn & Suites in Sacramento. An online search showed it gave all the appearances of being a trendy hotel. I'm sure being right next to the airport had something to do with that. Anyway, it was nice to see that the state was spending an extra buck on one of its employees.

CHAPTER 7

Like clockwork, there was a knock on my door at 8 a.m. It didn't catch me off guard. I had been prepared to leave for the past twenty minutes as I'm not one for tardiness. This time I didn't waste any time getting dressed and undressed into different sets of clothing. That drew a chuckle from me.

I threw my carry-on in the back seat and we were off. It took forty minutes to cover the fifteen-mile drive to the airport. We weren't going to break any speed records. That was for sure. The driver told me that the trip had gone actually better than expected. Welcome to Los Angeles, I mused.

Before we parted, he said he would be picking me up upon my return. That's good to know. I didn't need to provide him with any information about my return flight. He told me he would be sent my itinerary well ahead of time. Now I'm the one that felt like a droid.

My flight touched down at 10:50 a.m. I had an hour and ten minutes to get to the hotel, check in, clean myself up and be ready for pickup at 12 p.m. I felt that was cutting it a little close. Obviously, somebody really wants to get their money's worth out of me. Upon exiting the aircraft, I saw someone holding a sign in front of them over their head that read in large black lettering, JACK TOBACK. I couldn't have missed me if I tried. After getting his attention we strolled together toward the airport exit. Just outside and across the street was his company vehicle.

The ride from there to the hotel took no more than ten minutes. From the looks of it, I had a good forty-five minutes to spare before my scheduled pickup. There'd be plenty of time.

I hadn't eaten yet since last night and had a decent appetite, but instead, I crossed my fingers and hoped that there would be something served at this noontime orientation meeting. With that reasoning I wasn't about to hurry through a quick meal. I'll wait and see what they have.

With ample time on my side, I thought I'd give Irene a call at work. She picked up on the second ring. It was nice hearing her voice again. I caught her up on all of the latest. She seemed more excited about all of this going on than I was. She asked how long I would be in town. I said it's been tentatively scheduled for just three days.

She said, "Maybe one of these nights we could get together."

I replied "I wish. It looks like they're going to have me occupied from morning until late in to the evening."

She blurted out, "Damn."

"Yeah, I agree." I asked, "How's everything going at the mudhole?"

She snickered, "Since you left there haven't been any successful escapes yet."

I chuckled, "Thanks for putting my mind at ease. But on a more serious note, I've seen you in action and have total confidence in you."

In a low provocative tone, she whispered, "What do you mean by see me in action?"

We both laughed. I looked at the time and told her that I had only a couple of minutes to get downstairs.

She huffed, "Go man go." We said our goodbyes and clicked off.

When I got down to the lobby, I saw there was a car sitting just out front. It was the same driver as yesterday. Aren't these people ever late? I didn't need an invitation to know that it was for me. I got in the front seat again and we were off. We made the usual small talk and arrived at company headquarters in about twenty minutes. It took less time than I thought it would, traffic moved along well.

While sitting just outside the California Department of Corrections and Rehabilitation headquarters I was lost in reverie thinking back as I recalled my last visit here five years ago. It was for a mandatory meeting. From the outside it appeared that the place hadn't changed. Word got around that some significant changes had been made recently. Whatever modifications that had been done awaited me inside. I would soon find out.

At the check-in station inside I presented my ID and was handed a visitor badge and asked to take a seat. I attached it to my jacket.

By now my stomach was really talking to me. Peering down the hallway there were no vending machines in sight. Don't worry Jack, you're not going to faint.

Just then a woman walked up to me and extended her hand. As I got to my feet we shook and made our introductions. Her employee ID read Valerie Martinez, PhD. By all accounts she was not the coffee girl. It looked like I was finally going somewhere.

She led the way as I followed her into a new wing of the building. On my last visit here, this did not exist. She commented, "The wing we're in now was completed about two years ago. It took a couple of years to complete."

I was impressed with how everything was so modern and up-to-date compared to the rest of the building. We entered a door on the right.

The room was huge. Three of my condos could have easily fit inside. There were electronics of every type imaginable. I didn't know half the stuff I was looking at. Valerie guided me over to a desk at the other side of the room. The man sitting there saw us approach and got to his feet. She made the formal introductions.

"Mr. Director I would like you to meet Jack Toback. He is up here for training as the incoming Warden of Droid 1."

He stood and responded, "Jack we've been expecting you. Is it alright with you if I call you Jack?

I said, "Not a problem sir."

"Great, I'm Director Hillsdale. I'd appreciate it if you just called me Mitch."

I replied "Yes sir." It's going to take me some time.

"I know that we've run you around this morning quite a bit and I assume you haven't had a whole lot of time to stop and eat. Is that right?"

"That is correct. I could go for a bite." That was a real understatement. I didn't want to appear too desperate. In reality, I was famished.

He said, "That's good to hear. We have a buffet set up in the cafeteria. Let's go and have some lunch." On cue I began to salivate.

I replied, "That sounds good to me."

"You'll see the restrooms just before you hit the cafeteria. I'll see you inside."

"Alright Mit… Mr. Director." I didn't know if I'd ever be comfortable calling the director by his first name. I'm working on it.

When I walked into the cafeteria the smell was overwhelming. When you're hungry everything smells good right down to the greasy fries. The director caught my attention and waved me over to his table. There was an empty seat next to him. I saw a RESERVED sign on the table in front of my chair. It was all I could do to nonchalantly walk over there without rushing the buffet. I noticed that his chair was on my right. That's perfect, I'm a lefty. This way we won't be dueling with our elbows.

It was an excellent buffet. With a full belly and feeling like a human being once again we exited the cafeteria. When we reached his desk in the main room, he checked the time and said to me, "Jack, there's a short video that I want you to take a look at. In a nutshell, it describes a lot of what this operation is all about. You'll also have a manual to accompany the video and everything else that we will cover during your stay here. We call this manual the Bible. You'll need to learn it backwards and forwards. Valerie is going to be your guide during your time here. Do you have any questions so far?"

"None Director Hills - uh Mitch." Score one for Jack.

"Good. I'll have Valerie escort you over. It begins in about ten minutes. I'll talk to you later. Enjoy the show."

Not waiting for a reply, he turned and sat down at his desk and got back to work. I couldn't see an empty space anywhere on his desk. From out of nowhere Valerie appeared and led me towards the auditorium.

When we walked in it felt like I was at the movies. There must have been at least 200 seats. Valerie said that I could choose to sit anywhere I'd like. I chose somewhere around the middle, center.

She said, "The movie starts in a few minutes. I'll be back to get you when it's over. Have fun," she turned and left.

From the beginning, I could see that this was a professionally edited and directed production about the history of artificial intelligence right up to present day. It's amazing how far we've come in the last hundred years or so. I've seen documentaries before on artificial intelligence but never anything this instructive. When the lights slowly came back on, I glanced at the time and couldn't believe that it was a one-hour production. It felt more like fifteen minutes.

Valerie was waiting just outside the theater doors as I exited. I exclaimed, "Great presentation. There was only one thing missing."

"What was that?"

With a slight grin I said, "Popcorn."

She returned it with a slight smile and asked that I follow her. I felt like a puppy dog today. Next stop took me to the heart of the beast, the supercomputer.

It was monstrous and was described to me as no ordinary supercomputer. Its storage, speed of calculations and advanced processing algorithms placed it far above anything else out on the market. Years of research had gone into its improvement and design. It had been installed along one long wall. I estimated that there must have been 30 monitors that lined the wall above it.

I must have stood out like a sore thumb being the only one in the room not wearing a white lab coat. There were four, I assumed to be computer techs that were sitting at their stations in front of the monitors. These computer geeks it turned out were all at the doctoral level. The state invested in only the brightest and most qualified minds. That was a comforting feeling knowing we had the best that money could buy.

A signal was given and Valerie asked that I turn my attention to the monitor on the wall labeled 1. I took a seat and stared at the screen. Within a few seconds an image came up showing a prison cell with two inmates. Valerie asked me if I could tell the two apart. I couldn't at first but after a while I was able to detect the droid when the camera zoomed in for a closer shot.

I told her that after closer examination of the droid I found three distinct ways to identify it, him.

First, shining a light at their camera lens that took the place of pupils would be like shining one at a mirror, there's a strong reflection back.

Second, their skin was just too perfect, no wrinkles anywhere.

Last, the droid did not have our complex set of facial muscles. I could discern it when he tried to smile or frown. It was just a little off.

She said, "Excellent Jack. You're quite intuitive."

"Thank you, Valerie," I responded. It was nice to know that I had a cheerleader in my corner.

CHAPTER 8

A close inspection of the cell showed it to be a little bit larger than what I've seen before. Being roomier than most would provide more comfort for the inmate. There had to be a reason behind that. The two beds were on opposite sides of each other instead of being double bunked. Two barred windows above each of the beds faced outside. It had the usual sink and toiletry accommodations. Bars concluded the fourth wall of the cell, the entryway, the exit. As far as cells would go, this one would rate five stars.

The live video showed that they were both sitting on their bunks across from each other engrossed in conversation. Their body language appeared to be relaxed. The audio came in crystal clear. It was sitting right there in the same cell with them. I waited, watched and listened. Within a few minutes I came to understand that the conversation revolved around the inmate's life of crime. Some part of it anyway.

The droid sat on his bunk and didn't interrupt. Somehow, he genuinely seemed attentive to the conversation, more attentive than many humans I know. From the looks of it, I'd say that just the way he came across would put the inmate at ease. The droid was leaning slightly forward elbows on his knees, one hand wrapped over the other and placed just under the chin. The droid exuded the feeling that the only thing that mattered was listening to the inmate. He looked empathic. I was impressed.

Finally, the inmate paused and looked like he was waiting for a response. That's when the droid responded, "I see. How does that make you feel?" I couldn't have come up with a better response myself. Actually, I wouldn't have come up with *that* response.

After a long pause, the inmate muttered, "I guess I didn't think that one through very, much did I?"

The droid replied, "We all make mistakes John."

This was like sitting in on a counseling session. We continued to watch the interaction for another thirty minutes. It had moved along very well and had left me feeling that we were headed down the right road.

It must have been time for a coffee break because all the staff began moving as one. I was pulled along in a group all my own. My tour guide Valerie and I strolled back to the cafeteria. Inside coffee, tea, juice, water and various snacks were available. From the looks of my schedule in the manual received today, I could see I was going to be here for a long time. Caffeine and lots of it would be the beverage of choice. I opted for coffee with half-and-half. Valerie chose water. Still feeling satisfied from consuming a big lunch we chose nothing to eat to go along with our beverages.

I got right down to the heart of the matter. I asked her what her personal feelings were regarding the interaction between droids and humans.

She gave it some thought and said, "My education and training were in the field of Clinical Psychology. Everything written and studied was based upon human interaction only. There were no droid studies being offered anywhere other than here. This is new ground for me and we're on the cutting edge. We'll try as best to apply some of the basic rules and laws of psychology here between the droids and the inmates. It's going to be a learning process for everyone." After a long breath she smiled.

All of this certainly applies to me too. It looks like we're in the same boat. I asked her, "In your opinion, how long would it be expected to see positive steps made toward rehabilitation?"

She replied, "Jack I wish it was that simple. We'll be looking for benchmarks along the way."

I wasn't surprised to hear that. I knew that that was somewhat of a loaded question. She confirmed it.

She added, "As we learn more about these interactions, we'll be establishing new protocols that we will look to for guidance. All of the greatest minds of literature within this discipline have been input into the supercomputer. The list and its parameters are too long and complicated to go into specifics. All of these great tools are at our disposal. Many of us are confident that this will be successful. What percent success rate can I offer you? I can't tell you. I hope that answers at least one of your questions."

I said, "You've been entirely honest with me Valerie. In the future I hope to share your enthusiasm. From this point on only time will tell."

She nodded and looked at the time. "It looks like break is over."

According to schedule, it looks like my next planned visit will be at the Droid station. I had been looking forward to this particular workshop all day. It was time to see what my fellow employees were made of, literally.

Upon entering the spacious test lab, I noticed six droids that immediately caught my attention. Each one of them had been rotating around from different stations of testing. I couldn't tell one apart from the other right away. I suppose that didn't really matter. They were all dressed the same and of an identical height and build.

Valerie guided me over to our first stop, Station 1. It would be as good a place to start as any. This station had to do with the overall physical appearance of each droid. The technician went through a routine of measurements. This required checking and examining, in minute detail, each and every feature of the droid for quality assurance measures.

It was felt for the program to have its best chance for success the droids needed to appear as human-like as possible. I was informed that there's a new generation that's currently being worked on but won't be ready for some time yet.

The technician told us that artificial skin of varying shades covered their entire body. Hair length varied as well for the head and eyebrows.

High resolution cameras behind each orbit for the eyes gave them eyesight to die for.

Quality bidirectional microphones were embedded in each of their synthetic ear canals.

As could be plainly seen, their height and overall appearance were identical. I'd place them somewhere around medium build.

From my point of view, they could blend in anywhere with no difficulty. I had many questions but it was time to move on to Station 2. Looking ahead, my schedule showed I'd cover physical appearance more in-depth tomorrow. I'll hold my thoughts till then.

Our next stop along the way dealt with memory and responses. With the ever-advancing field of miniaturization, each of these droids was capable of storing and being able to call upon mountains of information. At this station they were being checked for recall by being prompted with various questions throughout a variety of different subjects. It was amazing how much information they held. Their responses were checked for accuracy. They'd be unbeatable on a game show.

This is where I couldn't help myself and decided to butt in. Some things are just too irresistible to pass up. I turned to Valerie and asked, "May I? I've got some questions of my own," as I gestured to the droid.

"Be my guest," she politely replied.

From where I sat, the droid and I faced each other from about three feet apart. After a little thought, I wanted to see if I could throw the droid off with an abstract question. First, I'd start off easy. I cleared my throat and asked, "Do you know who I am?"

The droid answered, "Yes, you are Jack Toback, the new warden at Droid 1. It's a pleasure to meet you."

I was taken back by his propriety. Well, I thought to myself almost anybody in the system would know that. Enough playing around, it was time for a real test, something a bit more profound.

I said, "Okay, tell me what life's all about."

The droid answered, "That's a pretty complex question Jack. Perhaps you would like to start."

That was all I needed to know. I felt like I was the one lying on a couch confessing my sins. I said, "Never mind." I decided that I'd asked enough questions for now. There'd be no putting anything over on this guy - droid. I've got to choose.

That wasn't exactly a scientific test but it told me that these electronic wonders are capable of not only recalling information but reasoning as well. I'll have to admit, I was impressed beyond doubt.

Scientifically, I imagine they'd call it performing many calculations with precision, extremely fast. It certainly got my undivided attention. I sat and observed as a technician went through various recall drills with the droid. Not a one was missed. It was time to move on.

At the next station we observed many of their sensory skills were being examined by a technician. For example, eye blinks were randomly programmed into each droid. That's something I would have never thought about. It's all a part of appearing human.

Thousands of miniature electronics were checked for varied forms of functioning under the skin of the droid's face. If the droid was told to smile, the technician would check for any irregularities against what an authentic smile would presumably look like. The technician told me that it was not perfect but close. Among other things, it's being worked on with a new generation of droids. The smile seemed almost completely natural to me but to the untrained eye there was no easy way to tell. Let's just leave it to the experts.

The artificial skin temperature of the droid was measured and recorded regularly. They did not want the internal temperature to register too hot. Overheating with most electronics has always been a concern. Ideally, it needed to be somewhere around 98.6. Once again, it was desired to be as close to human as possible. Thermal sub dermal implants would maintain the temperature as close to normal as possible. I learned that thousands upon thousands of these implants were placed all around its body. That in itself is quite an ingenious engineering feat.

The technician turned to me, noticed my rapt attention and asked, "How willing would you be to confide in someone who felt like an ice cube or an inferno?"

I came back, "Not much at all. That's a very good point. I get it. It's all about having human characteristics. That's been driven into my head since I first entered here." It all made perfect sense.

Valerie got my attention and began to stand. Apparently, it was time to wrap things up in the droid station for today. There is so much to learn here.

Dinner time was now upon us. Having skipped lunch, my appetite was in full swing. Valerie and I moved along with the crowd like a herd of cattle and made our way to the cafeteria. It didn't take long to find myself getting comfortable with this place.

The meal was served the same as lunch, buffet-style. That's talking my language. It was time to exercise a little more self-control. It wouldn't be necessary to eat like this would be my last meal. Either that or I'd be looking for larger size pants. I would be back in the morning. There'll be more food. Not to worry Jack.

After the evening meal I was assigned only one more activity for the day. That would be a lecture. It was like being back in school. The only difference being the absence of a final exam. Actually, I was enjoying myself. I never learned so much that I would soon be putting into use. The only difference between school and here, I was getting paid for it.

I'd say a group of us, maybe thirty found seats in the front of the lecture hall. This meeting hall was also big like everything else here. I'd say there were easily two hundred seats total, enough to qualify as a small theatre. After a few minutes, Director Hillsdale strode down the aisle, climbed up a few steps and took center stage behind a lectern. He was all smiles.

He first thanked us all for being here and recognized our dedication to the betterment of the penal system. He paused for a moment to allow for another manual that was being passed around to each of us. Between the two, I had enough reading material to last me for weeks.

After we quieted down, the Director asked us to open up to the first page of the manual. Shortly after that, an image was projected onto a screen directly in back of him. Before beginning his lecture, he asked us to hold all questions until the end of the session. He reminded us that a recording device, notepad and pen were supplied with each of the manuals. The subject matter ranged widely as we followed along in the manual.

I was unprepared for what was about to happen. Near the end, the director turned his attention to me and asked me to stand. Perplexed, I came to my feet. He turned back to the other guests and introduced me as the first warden who would assume control over Droid 1. After presenting a brief background of my experience I was received with a resounding applause. I even got a couple of whoops and whistles while I stood there like a dummy.

After the applause died down, I retook my seat. Someone sitting directly behind me leaned forward in his seat and whispered in my ear that he'd give anything in the world to change places with me. I shrugged my shoulders and smiled.

The lecture went on for another ten minutes before finally winding down. Everyone must have been exhausted. No one had any questions including myself. I couldn't believe it was already after 9 pm. It had been a long day but a beneficial one. There would be more to be resumed tomorrow.

CHAPTER 9

A different driver took me back to my hotel. There was no surprise there. It tells me at least the driver wasn't a droid I thought jokingly. I know that they can't obtain a license to operate a vehicle, not yet anyway.

When I got up to my room, I don't even remember getting undressed. I must have been asleep before my head hit the pillow. That was the best night's sleep I had in days, maybe weeks.

After waking and feeling totally refreshed, I washed, got dressed and met my driver promptly at 8:30 a.m. It was the same guy as yesterday. The way I'd been packing it away, I decided to hold off on breakfast and wait till lunch. My mom would have had a fit. She was a stickler for not missing meals. Sorry mom.

At the sign-in desk I was issued another visitor's pass. The one I wore yesterday I turned in upon leaving for the night. Once again, the same woman asked me to have a seat. You'd think I would have learned by now. According to today's agenda, I would be returning back to the droid section. I was looking forward to that.

Valerie showed up at 9:05 am. Finally, someone was late if even by only five minutes. As I stood, she apologized for having kept me waiting. I feigned disappointment. A convincing actor I'm not. She could see right through it. I shrugged my shoulders and tilted my head slightly down to the right, the universal sign for no problem.

As we headed toward the section, she asked how my evening went. I replied, "Uneventful. The moment I got to my room I fell into bed and slept like a log." That's about as far as our small talk went this morning. Caffeine was definitely first on the agenda.

It appeared that I finally made it. Today, I'd been given a white lab coat. It felt like I made it into the secret society. In honor of this occasion, I undid my pass and attached it to the outside of the lab coat.

Upon entering the room everything looked just as it had yesterday. Today would be in-depth training for one-to-one communication just between the droid and me. I had been especially waiting to getting my hands dirty here.

Valerie pulled a chair out for me and I graciously took a seat behind a keyboard with a monitor facing me from right in front. As she moved off to the side another white lab coat pulled up a chair and sat down next to me. Her ID badge announced that she was Doris Watson, PhD. I did everything in my power to resist saying, "Doctor Watson I presume?" I'm sure she's heard that a thousand times. We introduced ourselves. She came off as being friendly enough.

After introducing ourselves, she started by saying, "We feel the best way to learn this would be for you to actually execute the commands yourself, not watch me do it. It's felt that's the fastest and most efficient way to catch on. What do you think?"

I smiled and said, "I agree one-hundred percent Dr. Watson."

She returned my smile and said, "Doris will be just fine."

"Doris it is."

After shifting a little closer to the keyboard with my chair she said, "These basics are going to be the most important thing you'll learn today. They will be an everyday event when you return to your position at Droid 1. Okay, let's get started."

She glanced at the monitor then turned back to me. "Start by pressing the green button on the keyboard." After doing that the monitor came right up. Right after that she said, "At your facility in Pasadena you will have 4,000 cells. Each of them has a corresponding number that matches to the supercomputer there. Here we just have one cell labeled number 1. So, in this case just type the number 1 then press the blue command button."

Without hesitation I did so and the cell popped right up on the screen. So far so good, I'm at the skill level of a chimpanzee. I knew I had a way to go.

I noted that the same two occupants were in there from yesterday. Doris got my attention and pointed to a knob on the council that was labeled audio and said, "Turn that knob just a little clockwise." As I did the sounds from the cell came in louder and perfectly clear. Where they came in from, I don't know. There had to be some speakers hidden somewhere.

I commented, "That's great audio."

She said, "You haven't seen anything yet Jack, now comes the fun stuff. You're going to give the droid your first command."

"What will I be asking it, I mean him to do?"

"That's easy. First clip this wireless microphone on your lapel." It was tiny resting in the palm of her hand. After plucking it from her hand I clipped it in place. Doris mentioned, "When you toggle the M switch the microphone goes live but before you do that, I'd like you to think about what subtle physical move you would like the droid to do. Again, we're just working on simple instructions. This is part of your introduction into basic communication, nothing more. Please, don't ask the droid to do jumping jacks. Keep it simple," she said.

I thought for a moment and said, "Alright, I've got an idea."

She announced, "Toggle the switch, speak your command into the microphone and then toggle back again when you're done. The droid is the only one that will hear your command."

I responded, "That sounds easy enough. Okay, here goes." I cleared my throat and said, "Pick up your right hand and rub your chin gently with your thumb and forefinger." I watched as the Droid did exactly as told while never once breaking conversation. To me that was utterly amazing.

Doris spoke, "You just broke the ice. You're well on your way." With a smile and slight nod, I welcomed that. When I returned my eyes back to the screen, I could see the Droid was still rubbing his chin.

Doris saw my look of confusion and chuckled, "It's doing exactly as you instructed. Think about it."

After a moment I caught on and toggled the M switch and said, "Stop rubbing your chin" then toggled the switch again. The droid stopped immediately. This particular section could have been called Droid 101.

Doris led me through those sequences several more times with different instructions until it started to become automatic. It was just what I needed to kick start things. My confidence was growing.

She offered, "The lesson to be learned here is that he'll do exactly as instructed without question. Always remember that."

"I will." I said without any further question.

Just then Valerie caught my attention and had begun pointing her index finger at her open mouth, the universal sign that it was time for lunch. Stop the bus, I want to get off.

I caught sight of Director Hillsdale for the first time today inside the cafeteria. We made eye contact and he signaled me over. I'm glad I was already carrying a full tray of food in my hands. Having skipped breakfast, I was ravenous. I've had quite an appetite since I've been up here. Could it be the air? Sitting down beside him he turned and asked me how my morning had gone.

I told him, "It couldn't have gone better. From everything that's been introduced here it's turned out to be a great learning experience. I can assure you of one thing; it will be put to good use."

He seemed genuinely pleased with that remark. We got back to work on our food.

After lunch Valerie directed me over to the room labeled Physical 2. I soon discovered the purpose of this second room was to further measure the physical capabilities of the droids. Like all others, this room was cavernous. We walked over to the first station and Valerie introduced me to the technician. She politely asked that we sit down.

First up was strength. A sort of high-tech universal resistance system was stationed in the middle of the room that looked similar to those I'd seen in gyms. Only this had digital screens and readouts all around it. That's where the gym reference ended.

Upon given a signal, a droid approached the machine and got in to a supine position facing up on a bench. It was instructed to grab the bar on each side with both hands and press upward when instructed. I noticed that there were some wires attached to him at various areas around his body. They looked like sensors.

I passed on to Valerie, "This is a common bench-press. It's one of the best indicators of upper body strength."

"You know your weights Jack," she responded.

When the signal was given the droid acted and pressed the bar up with seemingly no effort then let it down slowly.

I said out loud, "That looked to me like it required little to no effort."

"It should have been. That was the equivalent of only 1,000 pounds," she smirked.

"Wow," slipped out of my mouth.

The resistance increased at the rate of 250 pounds at each succeeding press. I watched awestruck. The last bench press the droid successfully did was at 2,500 pounds which just so happened to reach the maximum capacity of the machine. Readouts were taken at each of the presses. These revealed the droid's internal structures and how much stress was being applied to each. It was determined that the last press was all the droid was safely capable of doing.

I wish I had the capability of doing one tenth of that. A similar test was performed for leg strength with similar supernatural results. I couldn't believe the strength that this droid possessed. Put a football jersey on him and he's ready to go. Training camp wouldn't be necessary. He'd be unstoppable.

Our next stop was vision. A different droid was asked to read five lines on a screen that was about twenty feet away. With each successful pass, the size of the font was reduced. The test continued until it was deemed successful.

From where I was seated which was the same distance away, it looked like the screen contained no characters at all. Curiosity got the better of me. I walked up to it and squinted to see that the letters were tiny. They couldn't have been larger than a sixteenth of an inch in height. These droids must have the eyesight of an eagle. Their capabilities are mind boggling.

Next stop along the way took us to a station with seats that faced a treadmill. It was longer than a typical one and had built in sensors and digital readouts all along it. The technician spoke into the same type of microphone I used yesterday. After a couple of minutes, the star of the show came over. This station would serve as an evaluation for the test of leg stamina and speed. Without being instructed, the droid stepped onto the treadmill and waited. The technician signaled to us that the test would now begin.

The belt of the machine began to move slowly at first. Our robotic friend responded with a casual walking pace in response. The speed gradually increased. Now it was moving at a fast walk. It easily kept pace as the degree of upward incline went to a challenging 30 degrees. After five minutes it came down to horizontal then moved down to a decline of 30 degrees. That would be a steep downhill. All presented no problem. It was a marvel to watch in action.

The level returned back to horizontal as the speed increased. From my vantage point I could see the digital readout showed that the belt was moving at 20 miles per hour. That works out to a three-minute mile. There appeared to be no problem whatsoever with keeping pace. It held that brisk pace for a few minutes. The speed continually increased. After a while, the legs of the droid began to look like a blur.

According to the readout, it was running smoothly at a speed 60 miles per hour. I could hardly believe my eyes.

The capacity of the treadmill has been reached. Increases and decreases in elevation were added at that speed then returned back to horizontal. They were all taken in stride. After a few minutes the belt began to slow. Shortly it came to a complete stop. The humanoid showed no signs of exhaustion, sweating or pain, of course no sweating. Actually, he looked exactly the same as when he first stepped on. Electronic measurements were taken and showed no signs of stress or injury anywhere within its internal structures. Superman would be envious.

I turned and said to Valerie, "It's remarkable. Can you imagine casually running long distance at 60 miles per hour? My money's on this guy."

What appeared to be our last stop was a hearing evaluation. The droid was sitting in a small sound booth and told to press a button when it heard a sound through the headphones. The test was run automatically. When it had been completed, an audiogram was produced showing the results. I've had hearing tests before but I wasn't familiar with these results.

It was explained to me in simple layman's terms that a droid would be able hear someone playing a violin from as far as five miles away. That sounded on par with supernatural hearing. I commented, "There'd be no talking about him behind his back." Valerie laughed.

At the time all I could think to say was, "I'm blown away. By human standards, these droids are certainly not wimps."

I had one more stop for the day. It would be back to the auditorium for another lecture. Only this would turn out to be a long one. Dinner would be served at sometime around the middle of the presentation.

Director Hillsdale was already seated at a table on stage while we were finding our seats. Just after being seated another manual was being passed around for each of us that also contained memory sticks, note pads and pens.

I glanced around and still didn't understand everyone's purpose for being here but that didn't concern me. As far as I was concerned, all this was just for me. I wanted to grasp as much of this as I could. In practice I'd need every bit of it real soon.

The topics today ranged from troubleshooting the droids to running performance tests on the supercomputer, administrative duties, financial record keeping and increasing public goodwill and confidence, quite a load.

As scheduled somewhere around halfway through we broke for dinner. We had a full hour. I'll say one thing about the people here in Sacramento, they sure know how to put out a spread. I'm glad that dinner was restricted to one hour otherwise I'd still be sitting there stuffing my face. Only another hour and a half remained of lecture. I'll do my best to stay awake.

At the second half, the star of the show was brought in, a droid. He positioned himself next to the director. This section we learned was going to be interactive. That's just what was needed. Not only we would be the ones asking questions but so would the droid.

The banter went on back and forth. I can't say there was anything about the interaction that I did not enjoy. This droid seemed more than capable of controlling any scenario presented to it. It gave me a real sense of confidence knowing that they'd be on my side. Tomorrow would conclude my training. Pity, I was just getting to like it up here. I suppose that the buffet had something to do with that.

CHAPTER 10

The last day of Droid School was upon me. From my perspective, it felt that I had really covered the meat and potatoes during the first two days up here. How much more new information could they possibly throw at me? Most importantly, how much of it would stick?

There were some new facets of the droid study I read about in the manual that would be covered today, but for the most part, today would be dedicated to review – review – review. I'm an advocate for that way of learning. Realistically, there's no way anyone can grasp all that I've experienced in the last few days. In my opinion, the reviews will be great for topping everything off.

Today's agenda was titled One-to-one. For the first time, I'd actually be on the front lines. That meant individual cell time with the inmate and droid.

Zero hour was set for 10 a.m. I had been reminded by Valerie to interact in the way I found most helpful. That left a lot open to interpretation.

She said in a low voice, "Just be you."

Before going in I glanced at the file of the inmate, John Carpenter. He had been sent up for the transportation of illegal narcotics. It's an offense I've seen ruin thousands of lives over the years. I opted

not to read any further into his file. This time I
decided to let the chips fall where they may. Up to
this point it had all been academic. I wanted
everything about this interaction to be on a level
playing field. I'd have no hometown advantage.

My trusty guide, Valerie, would not accompany
me on this planned visit. I was on my own. A map
was given me that displayed the location of the
holding cell. It was set off by itself at the end of a
long corridor.

After passing through a sound proof door, I
continued my journey along the hallway as directed.
It didn't take long; there it was on the left. I stood
before the bars.

I cleared my throat and announced, "John, my
name is Jack Toback. I'm part of the prison system
here in California." There was no answer.

"Would it be okay if I came in to talk?"

John stood up from his bunk. "Yes sir," he replied.

Obviously, I was under close surveillance as only
seconds later the bars to the cell opened. After I had
taken a few steps inside, there was John. He was
standing before me with his hand extended. My hand
greeted his and we shook. Nice start, I thought. My
first impression suggested to me that he's not exactly
the gangster type. Starting things off, I was already
impressed. He was alone in the cell. I asked, "Where
did your cellmate go?" I didn't say droid.

George was called away," he said.

The way he said it made it sound like they were
good friends.

He motioned to George's bunk and said, "Please have a seat sir."

"Thank you."

We both took our seats at the same time. I glanced around the cell. It was nicer than any other I've seen with the exception of Droid 1. They're identical.

Turning my attention back to John, I asked, "If it's okay with you, I'd like to hear about your experience within the prison system. Feel free to tell me anything you'd like. You won't be penalized for anything you say. This will be all off the books."

John lowered his head and sat motionless for a few minutes. I wasn't going to break the silence.

Finally, he raised his head and said, "Just after I graduated from High School I got involved with the wrong crowd. Clearly, I know that now."

He said, "On a lot of days we senselessly wasted time by hanging out, smoking pot and drinking beer. That was the first time I ever smoked."

He looked at me and I nodded.

"Then one night, one of the guys, Tommy, asked the group in general, "Is there anybody here interested in making some easy money? From what I heard it's not small potatoes." A hush came over all of us.

Then one of the guys, Brad, got everyone's attention.

"What'd you have in mind?"

He was the oldest one, somewhere around thirty.

Tommy said, "A friend of mine knows someone who needs to transport some product from San Diego to San Francisco. It's as simple as that."

I had a pretty good idea of what was meant by the word *product*. With my big mouth I had to ask, "How much is in it for me?"

Tommy replied, "I don't know. You'll have to talk to the guy about that."

Again, stupid me wouldn't give up and come to my senses, so I asked, "When can we meet?"

"I don't know, but I'll get back in touch with him and see if he can put together a meeting with you. When I hear back, I'll let you know."

I gave Tommy my phone number. Doing that would turn out to be the colossal mistake of my life. My head was not screwed on properly.

Three days later Tommy called. He said that the guy would meet with me at a special place and time in Balboa Park. It was close to home. I agreed.

When I got there, I sat down at the designated bench. It was easy to find. The thought occurred to me, where were the other guys, my so-called friends? Was it just me doing this?

Something didn't feel quite right. There was a voice inside me pleading to get the hell out of there. In hindsight, I should have listened.

I was debating about leaving when a stranger sat down at the other end of the bench. I had a feeling it might be the guy. I'd put him somewhere around forty. He looked over at me and asked my name.

After telling him he slid over closer to me. I never got his.

He said that my job was to pick up a package from someone in San Diego and transport it to an address in San Francisco, no questions asked. Upon its arrival, I would be compensated in the amount of five-thousand dollars. He questioned, "Are you in or out?"

The lure of that much money at one time was just too much to turn my back on. I was almost broke and couldn't ask my parents for another dime. Then I made my forever life-changing mistake.

Without giving it any further thought, I said, "When can I start?" Those four words sealed my fate.

"To make a long story short, as you already know, I never made it as far as San Francisco. I was arrested at a check point along interstate 5 about halfway there. To this day, I still can't believe I did such a stupid thing." John began to shake his head and lowered it into his hands.

I said, "You don't have to go on if you don't want to." I didn't expect him to be so forthcoming.

After a short pause he said, "You wanted to know about my prison experience. I'm coming to it now."

I didn't say anything and nodded for him to continue.

"Being a first-time offender, the judge let me off with a minimum three-year sentence with the possibility of parole. It still sounded like a lifetime to me. My parents were devastated. There was nothing I could say to them. I was sentenced to serve my time in Monroe State Prison."

I said, "I know of the place."

"After serving about a year of my sentence there, I was quickly learning how to be an accepted gang member. Being alone in jail made you vulnerable, an easy target. That had to change if I was to survive. It was all about trying to keep myself in one piece. I was on the road to nowhere."

I said, "I understand where you're coming from," and fell silent.

"About six months ago, I was transferred to this correctional facility. I haven't seen any other prisoners since my time here, just my cellmate, um friend, George. Yeah, I spotted some little things about him that told me he's not human. I don't know what this is all about and frankly I don't care. But do you want to hear something funny? I'd rather talk with him than any one else I've ever known. He gets me."

John sat up straighter. "If you don't mind, I'd like to say one more thing. George has convinced me that upon my release, continuing my education would be a step in the right direction. With his help we've even gotten hold of several college catalogs and schedules and are in the process of considering enrollment once my sentence is up."

John went on, "There are many other positive things about me he's brought out that have entirely turned my life around. And I'll prove it to my parents, the prison system and most importantly *me* when I get out. For the first time in my life I have a direction."

I couldn't believe that I was hearing all of this coming from the mouth of a twenty-year-old convict, young man. From what little I heard, I thought that John would have potential to go far in this world. I've always prided myself on being a good judge of character. I'd bet his recent perspective of life was at the hands of George, his droid mentor. Score one for the droids.

My time was up. We shook hands one more time as I wished John all the luck in the world upon his release. The cell doors opened and closed upon my exit.

I'd have to say that this encounter actually turned out to be one of the most productive times I've had here. It was an all hands-on experience that gave me a sneak preview of what was to come. Essentially, it allowed me to witness how the whole program would eventually come together. I could visualize it in action in a much larger scale and liked what I saw.

Confidence about the strength of this program exuded from me from what I'd learned during my intensive three days up here. I was eagerly looking forward to returning to Pasadena to put some of these newly acquired skills to use.

The day had finally come to an end. I thanked Director Hillsdale and Doctors Valerie Martinez and Doris Watson for their guidance and support. They each in turn gave me their card and said I could call them anytime.

Valerie said, "Don't hesitate to call even if it's not work related." That was nice of her, I thought.

CHAPTER 11

Next morning, I was on my way back to Pasadena, and it couldn't have come a minute too soon. Be it ever so humble…

After gathering my mail, I walked through the front door sometime around late morning and was free to enjoy the rest of the day on my own. I could live with that. After showering off the remains of Sacramento, I thought I'd give Irene a call.

When she answered I asked, "How are things going in the rock quarry?"

That's all I could come up with at the time. It's always nice to hear her voice.

"I was hoping to hear from you today. From what you told me, three days in training and you're done. So, I assume you're home."

I replied, "Got back not too long ago. You know, it's like what a professor had once told me years ago in college. He said, 'When you leave here after completing four years of school and getting your degree, if you feel like you didn't learn anything, then you know you've had the perfect education.' Now I can appreciate what he was truly talking about."

I filled Irene in on what we had covered. She was amazed we had gone over so much material in just three days. I asked her how the job was going. She said it had been going as well as expected speaking of which she had to get off the phone, duty called. We said our goodbyes and disconnected. Too bad she's so far away. Our time will come.

It was repeatedly drilled in class that with the introduction of droids, there would be no further interactions among inmates. That meant none at all. For all of us that had been in the penal system for years, that would take some getting used to.

This alone had been one of the main reasons for introducing droids to prison reform. For many years it was shown time and again that commingling among the inmates proved to be the root cause of all problems in prison. Eliminate those interactions and we rid the jails of the never-ending gangs, drugs, violence, and sexual assaults. It would be like a dream come true.

Most of the time the droid would spend with the inmate would be in the cell together. Meals and the one-hour exercise period would be accomplished separately. The droids would even bring back food from the cafeteria to their cellmates. It was not necessary for any of the inmates to venture down there.

This would be an amazing first, never before had such a radical step been implemented. The inmates would never come into contact with each other even when they would go for the one hour of exercise a day. The droids would be their sole companion for the length of their sentence.

Within the state legislature it was unanimously agreed upon that incarceration was not intended to be a sleep away camp. For too many criminals it meant do your time, make your connections and come out a better gangster. Even for those that avoided the gangs and violence, none had come out the better for their confinement. It was a no-win situation.

It was these early rumblings that echoed inside the penal system ages ago that inspired the introduction of artificial intelligence. It was thought that the introduction of the droids would be an alternative for a shortcut to rehabilitation, so it was hoped. There was only one way to find out.

Having a humanoid of super intelligence as your cellmate would be like having a walking talking super intelligent friend at your disposal just for the asking. That was an important part of the plan.

The droid needed to be well versed in virtually, everything. The exchange of information though needed to be in a fair and honest dialogue. It had to be two ways. Even though the droid knew the answers to anything asked, it would on many occasions feign ignorance and ask the cellmate of his opinion or answer.

With all the intricately stored data on the cellmate, the object would be to get inside his head, learn about him and make inroads toward rehabilitation. It was a simple plan. I suppose, some might compare this to brainwashing. In a case like ours, it might be more appropriately referred to as *brain cleansing*.

Depending upon its effectiveness, it was hoped that the inmates would in many cases be released early. The droids would be an integral part of the system performing psychological tests to their unaware cellmates and grading them as they spent quality time together. The results with potential recommendations for those in line for parole would be passed along to other officials and experts in the department.

Seeing as how this is a pilot field study of a unique nature, a new baseline would be established for determining complete or near complete rehabilitation. That would be the obvious gray area of the entire study.

With everything in place, the ones who were calling the shots felt comfortable that the odds were stacked heavily in their favor. Most felt confident that this program would prove successful. I'll admit it rubbed off on me as well.

As learned from part of my hands-on experience in Sacramento, every evening while the inmates slept the droids would wirelessly download from the cell to the main supercomputer in the prison all the communications of the day.

The most advanced form of voice recognition would determine intonation, pitch, pauses and speed of delivery.

For much of the analysis human interaction was not necessary. The supercomputer could do it all. It was truly analytical.

Video analysis of face recognition would determine any tells that might suggest lying on the part of the inmate. There are dozens of muscles in the face that work like a lie detector when someone is not telling the truth. These would remain recorded in the droid's memory. A seasoned detective is skilled in this area of interrogation. Droids would also be in possession of this valuable skill.

This information along with the inmates file would establish tomorrow's planned approach with each and every droid. The program was always looking ahead and planning out the next day.

The supercomputer would download instructions to the droid of what remedy or actions might best be taken. These instructions would be carried out to the letter without question. Everything that could have been thought of was. How could it possibly miss?

Traditionally, during mealtime was when many of the fights and drug deals had gone down. This was one of the major roadblocks to rehabilitation. It made all the sense in the world, eliminate those encounters and you eliminate the problems. It was as simple as that. There could be no arguing that point. In fact, no inmate contact was the ultimate goal. There was really nothing to lose and everything to gain.

My prison had it arranged for an hour of exercise to occur at seven different one-hour intervals that ranged from 10 a.m. to 5 p.m. The exercise yard was huge. At full capacity, 572 inmates would be out for their exercise hour at any of the one-hour intervals.

The prison yard was fenced off with as many individual enclosures and even a few more. Solid construction along each fenced lot made it impossible for inmates to see or talk to each other. In other prisons this was the only other time when inmates were able to congregate. That wasn't going to happen here.

Each fenced off location was the size of a tenth of an acre. That would be 4,356 square feet or a simpler way of looking at it, 50 by 87 feet. It allowed for plenty of room to move about. Even jogging would not be out of the question. Each spot even included ample exercise equipment.

On many occasions the droid would accompany the inmate if invited. More bonding was the ultimate goal. Everything so it seemed had been thought of and was in place. It seemed to me that that rehabilitation was already a forgone conclusion.

Data that had been gathered for the inmates would be sent daily to the state and federal government for further analysis. Everybody had their eyes glued to Droid 1.

There'd be constant communication with the brightest minds in the fields of prison reform and psychology. They would be following the results closely and offering their opinions as needed. There was a lot riding on this project. Failure was not an option. It couldn't happen.

Most of the day-to-day operations would take place automatically. There were scheduled frequent tests of the supercomputer to see that all systems were running perfectly. I know my way around computers fairly well but this monster goes well beyond Windows 36.

Part of my duties would entail that I would oversee inmate transport to and from the prison.

A manual will guide me through general troubleshooting for droid maintenance and repair. If and when the time comes that they're down, we have extra droids that are ready to go as replacements. That's what I call good planning. Anything that can possibly go wrong usually does in time. That's my old way of thinking and it's gotten me this far.

The criterion that was used for choosing inmates for Droid 1 was based on several factors. Taken into account was the nature of their crime, current age, and years remaining on their sentence.

It was realized early on that some of the worst offenders were out of reach for rehabilitation no matter what resources were used. There would be no turning them around.

These were usually the convicts sent up with long sentences for crimes such as murder one, kidnapping, drug importers, sexual predators and those with mental illness. Speaking of mental illness, the public is not generally aware of the fact that all prisons contain a large population of the mentally ill. That's rather sad.

Any prisoner over the age of 35 was not considered to be a worthwhile investment for this program. It was thought, the younger the better. A line had to be drawn somewhere.

Those with one to three years left on their sentence were considered to be ideal candidates. I don't know how they arrived at that conclusion. It wasn't touched on in class. My guess would be that it might have had something to do with their age and type of offense.

Those were the parameters that the prison commission based its incoming prison population of Droid 1 on. It was their best guess and would always be subject to change as the pilot study progressed.

Again, this was a huge first in the penal system. So, they had to establish a baseline somewhere. Me, I did what I had always had done and supported the system to the letter. The fewer waves the better.

CHAPTER 12

When inmates first began arriving many of them resented having non-humans as cellmates though there were those that took it in stride. I'd say that it was split right down the middle, 50-50.

The complainers made their feelings well-known to the outside world and to anyone else who would listen. Like a raging wildfire, the media quickly grabbed the attention that had been pouring out of from all the restless machinations going on inside the prison walls. One tabloid headline that followed the story read INMATE AND LAB RAT. As predicted, it met with mixed reactions among the public.

Their voices reverberated throughout the United States and the world. This sparked intense debate among some groups that were filled with hatred for the penal system - authority.

One of them had rallied at the gates of the prison 5,000 strong with protest signs that read END INDIGNITY NOW. It all seemed so deplorable to me. Did these people forget that behind these gates' criminals are housed inside?

Dissension appeared to be wavering among the inmates. It appeared that the tide was shifting in favor of the change. Fewer of them were opposed to having non-humans as cellmates. In fact, many had thought that it was pretty cool. Others actually appreciated not having to deal with the thugs, drugs and fear of being raped. Everyone here intimately knows what goes in prison. From the front row seat where I spent many years of my life, I could certainly understand that.

As the weeks went by, inmates continued to roll in by the busload. After only one month the prison contained 800 inmates. The program was seriously underway. We were even a little ahead of schedule for reaching full capacity by six months. In a memo I read, the governor was pleased with the way it was going. He should be.

This was the quietest time I had ever spent as warden in a prison. It was all so surreal. If I didn't know better, it was almost as if I wasn't in a jail at all. What an amazing change. It was almost like being in a retirement home. There were no fights, stabbings, drugs or rapes. There's no prison that could make such a claim, none whatsoever. All hopes for success seemed to be falling neatly into place.

I randomly screened the interactions between the droids and their cellmates. Those that resented the droids at first eventually appeared to be making headway with them as time rolled on. This was reminiscent of the time I spent with the inmate John when I was training in Sacramento. He had turned himself around. With the droid's support, I was beginning to see that here as well. It was working.

It was soon discovered that many of the inmates had a great respect for the droids' strength. I watched with delight as many of the larger, beefier inmates challenged their droid cellmate to an arm-wrestling contest. The outcome though was always predictable and amusing.

We had been operational for just a little more than a month when the first of the usual threatening messages started coming in. Most are delivered through the prison email system. I had seen this time and time again. It was nothing new to me. It all went with the job. My only surprise was that it took so long to finally start. It might have taken longer to get going because this program is new.

All threats no matter how minor is taken seriously and cannot go undocumented. I had to file each and every one and send duplicates up north. In short order I got better at screening out the ones that were from people who were just venting as opposed to the ones with a more serious agenda. Again, it always comes down to experience.

There was one message in particular that stood out clearly from the rest. For one, the voice was indistinguishable. Many times, I could tell if it was local or from a particular part of the state or country. In this case, I couldn't even distinguish if this one was domestic or foreign. I didn't have a clue. That would be up to the dark net boys up north to determine its origin. That's how things are handled – by the book. It was out of my hands and glad of it too.

This particular message stated that our operation did not conform to the general support and approval of the general public. It went on further to say that we were in direct conflict with the constitution. There were no statutes quoted. It further went on to state that our presence may be challenged in the Supreme Court. That's really taking quite a leap.

Since receiving the message, the dark net team in Sacramento had maintained constant contact with me. Not a frequent occurrence, they'd hit a stone wall and hadn't been able to yield any information yet on the source of the threats.

One of the hackers told me, "It looks like we're up against someone who knows how to hide their tracks really well. So right away that tells us that this is no rank amateur. That heightened our suspicions up to the next level. For the present time, all I can tell you is we're working on it."

Those weren't the most reassuring words to hear.

It was quiet for about a week. No further messages from the sender had come in. As what happens with some, maybe they lost interest in pursuing it any further.

Then suddenly, the silence was broken. A new message was received. Whoever sent it threatened that if we don't cease operations soon, we'd be headed on a collision course with disaster.

That was the first real threat that had been issued which carried intended consequences. According to the IT team, the threat level just got pushed up another notch.

In particular, what gave me general reason for concern was that the sender identified our supercomputer, make and model, and not only just that, serial number too. There are only a handful of people with access to that guarded information. Whoever was behind this was well informed, too well.

Personally, I now began to take these threats much more seriously. So, did Sacramento. Someone or some group had handily infiltrated our secure system. Still our rifle squad of IT professionals could not offer up any solutions and what made that especially worrisome was that they were highly skilled and were some of the best.

The threats continued on, but only now they began to outline what our present prison population was and how many new inmates would be arriving in the next few days. There was no way anyone outside the prison system could possibly have access to this information.

We'd already been over this. We knew that it was limited to only the few top people in charge. Might there be a mole operating somewhere inside? I'm sure that avenue is already under investigation. Someone was making a clear statement to us implying that they had us over a barrel. It was like someone was laughing right in our faces. What else could this one individual possibly be capable of? I can't begin to imagine.

I knew it was coming. An ultimatum from the sender had been proclaimed. The next threat spelled out in no uncertain terms that when maximum capacity of the prison had been reached, brutal action would be taken. How or by what means was not mentioned. That left everything up to the imagination.

My first thought was a bomb. Typically, bomb threats were among the most usual though few are carried out. All I, all we could do was hope that these threats were nothing more than that. For the most part many turn out to be a hoax. We'd have to find out the hard way. Only time would tell.

Just to be on the safe side, the presence of increased security had been ordered and had been gradually building up around the prison. It was unknown what type of attack if any would be brought against the prison. Any vehicle approaching the prison was stopped and thoroughly searched.

The prison system in California along with the rest of the country, the world, was completely unprepared for what was about to happen. It was just around the corner and would be far worse than any worst-case scenario imagined.

Droid 1 had now been in operation for almost six months. Slightly ahead of schedule, the prison had just recently reached its maximum capacity of 4,000 inmates. It would turn out to be a bittersweet accomplishment.

Every day since the threats began coming in, I'd been walking on thin ice. There was something about the way they were written that unnerved me. The voice of the threats did not carry the usual emotional outcries that many had.

Now it was only a matter of time to see if the sender of those threats would deliver as promised on them. Call it intuition, for some reason, something inside me screamed in my ear that he would. There's been times before when I've misconstrued the meaning of previous threats. This was one time when I was hoping to be wrong, once again. There was nothing that any of us on the front lines could do about it but just sit and wait. That's the toughest part.

CHAPTER 13

It was only after the fact that we learned sometime during the early morning hours someone had hacked into the supercomputer's main terminal at Droid 1. Up in Sacramento, the dark net crew said it couldn't be done. Well, it was.

With all its redundant firewalls and built in protections it was deemed to be impenetrable. All possible safeguards to eliminate illegal entry were in place.

The nightmare unfolded while I and most of the population on the West coast were still fast asleep. If I could live to be one thousand, it would turn into a morning I'd never forget.

The attacker gained entry to the supercomputer during the early morning hours and once inside had complete access to everything including all internal communication with the droids. He knew what he was doing and where he was headed. Apparently, many hours, perhaps days of preparation went into this cyber attack of the worst kind.

It would later be revealed that at precisely 3 a.m. orders were issued to all droids that would ultimately prove fatal for all the inmates.

It was discovered that the instructions given the droids demanded that at precisely 5 a.m. they would terminate their cellmate, all four-thousand of them. An unprecedented mass murder had been ordered.

For those of us that worked close with the droids, we all knew that they had been programmed to follow instruction without deviation no matter what it was. Sadly, they did. It was shortly after 5 a.m. that not a single inmate was left alive. It was the most massive serial killing on American soil.

It didn't take long to for the media to get wind of it. Not pulling any punches, the first tabloid to hit the market read: FOUR-THOUSAND INMATES BRUTALLY MURDERED. Emergency broadcast signals had it on every news channel across the nation. In a matter of minutes, it spread to every news outlet around the world.

It was bewildering that the media had this information as quickly as we did. We're right here at ground zero. This had been a coordinated attack with little time for us to react. All prisoners died of strangulation or an apparent broken neck. The medical scanners in each cell indicated that none of the inmates had a pulse or signs of brain activity. Death came quickly.

The penal system was paralyzed. America was in shock. This was the greatest tragedy that the United States has ever suffered, all at the hands of potentially just one person. This heinous act of terrorism had caught the attention of the entire world by storm. Here at home, the penal system had ground to a standstill.

A deep impact was felt from the penal system throughout the state. Riots had broken out within many prisons. No one was prepared for that. Dozens of correctional officers had been heartlessly murdered in retaliation for Droid 1.

The National Guard had been activated. The military had been called in. Scores of prisoners died while trying to repel their attack. The devil had finally come to roost.

There's no way to prepare for something as heinous as this. Nothing in any of my manuals, not a single time during my twenty years of service addressed anything like this.

At headquarters in Sacramento, no one could offer any advice. Everyone up there was dumbstruck. My many calls to the governor for help went unanswered. Where was he when I needed him?

Meanwhile, inside my prison walls I had 4,000 dead bodies beginning to decompose in their cells. I walked the halls and was utterly sickened by the sight. Lifeless bodies were everywhere. Even the droids seemed sympathetic to what they had done. There was nothing I could say to any of them.

What was I going to do with all the dead? The sheer number of them is staggering. That was a question that went way beyond my pay grade.

And what's to be done with the droids? I didn't know where to begin. Did anyone?

The dire logistics proved outrageous. It would take an endless array of ambulances miles long to carry away the bodies. That is if anywhere near that number could be obtained right away. That would be impossible.

Ordinarily, due to the nature of their death's, autopsies would also need to be performed. What's more, where would all the bodies be stored? As I saw it, there's no way that's going to happen. It was an appalling mess of immeasurable proportion.

It was just then the feeling came over me that I'd been abandoned. I was the only live soul remaining within these prison walls. Was I just imagining it? I got the feeling that everyone had already deserted the sinking ship, while I'd been thrown under the bus.

Inwardly, I knew it was only a matter of time before many eyes would fall upon me, the scapegoat. From many years experience, I knew that many grief-stricken friends and family, and those with a burning dislike for authority would hold me responsible for this tragedy. I felt like I was standing before a firing squad. Somebody had to be the fall guy.

Essentially, my life from this moment on wasn't worth a whole lot. I had to do something and do it soon before it was too late. Time to dwell on this would not act favorably for me. It was time to make a run for it.

Just after I got home as if right on cue my phone rang. Caller ID showed it to be Irene. What could I possibly say to her? I thought about letting it go to voicemail but answered on the last ring.

All I could muster up was, "Hello Irene."

Clearly choked up she said, "Jack, I hardly know what to say. How are you holding up down there?"

I could hear the anguish in her voice. I struggled to barely get it out, "I'm not! It's only a matter of time till someone or most likely a mob comes for me. They're going to want real blood, not droid circuitry. You know how this works. I'm the most convenient one to lash out at and the closest. I'm a dead man walking." I couldn't sugarcoat it.

After a moment's pause, she screamed into the phone, "The hell they will! Where are you now?"

"I just got home a little while ago. The street's still clear in front of my condo but I don't think for much longer."

She said, "Listen carefully. Here's the plan. Pack up your stuff, just clothing. Get in your car and take the 5 north. Don't stop for anything along the way. Don't use any of your credit cards. Disconnect your phone. Don't use the GPS. Use a paper map if you need to. You want to be a ghost. You know where I live. I will be expecting you. No arguments. Just do it now!" she demanded.

I said, "But we don't even..."

She stopped me mid-sentence, "Stop right there. Pack up your stuff. Do it now or do I have to come down there and get you?! I will!"

I replied, "I'm almost on my way."

She said, "Have a safe trip honey. I'll be waiting," she disconnected.

I almost can't believe I'm doing this. I've been down here six months and now I feel like I'm on the run like a common fugitive. I resented being left high and dry or was it just my imagination running away with itself? This has all happened so quickly. I haven't had time to think. Anyway, there was no sense in going over that again. It won't do me any good at this time.

In addition to clothing and some personal items, I packed a sandwich, a bag of chips and some water for the road. It was going to be a long trip. After 45 minutes I was ready to leave. I looked around and made a silent goodbye to my surroundings. I left my blinds cracked just a little so I could see outside in front. One last look would confirm that the coast was clear. It wasn't.

From my vantage point, I saw a dark sedan parked on the other side of the street. Inside I could make out the silhouettes of what looked like three people inside, all male. There were two in the front, one in the back. What were they doing just sitting there? That was an easy one. They were probably waiting to gun me down. It was payback time.

There was no plan B. I would have to come up with one on the spot. I'll need to call Irene and tell her I may not be able to make it. While planning my parting words out for her I kept my eye on the sedan. Just before making the undesired call, to my relief, someone came from one of the condo units and approached the sedan, opened the back door and got in.

After no more than a few seconds the car sped off. I let out a sigh that probably could have been heard on the other side of town. I didn't know how much longer my luck would hold out. I was breathing on borrowed time. Maybe that was an omen that the time to leave was right now. I listened to it.

Just after the car got out of sight, I exited my condo and swiftly carried my baggage to my car. It took two trips. In my haste to pack the trunk, everything fit tightly in it. I had to sit on it to get it to close.

My impromptu disguise consisted of a baseball hat and sunglasses. That's the best I could come up with on short notice. I could see that my car batteries were almost fully charged. That would be plenty of juice to get me safely up north. Sitting behind the wheel, I took one last look at my condo on my right and inaudibly said my goodbyes to my former life. I pulled out of my spot and headed toward Interstate 5. I thought could this be construed as leaving the scene? I shook my head and realized I'd rather be alive. As the old saying goes, *I'd rather be tried by twelve than carried by six.*

It dawned on me, before I left town, I had the good sense to stop at my bank and drain the last dollar out of my checking and savings accounts. I was in and out with no questions asked. Somehow it was amusing, but I felt like I was on America's most wanted list.

Paranoia was beginning to seep into my bones. The more miles I put between myself and Pasadena the better and safer I'd feel. Goodbye Southern California. Goodbye career.

It's amazing how the world, make that my world can change in the blink of an eye. In all my days, I never thought that I would ever get blindsided like this. Overnight I'd gone from respected Warden to a perceived killer on the run. It's still difficult to wrap my head around all this, just keep driving.

I'd been heading up Interstate 5 for about two hours now, and all these thoughts are continually flying through my head. What could I have done to prevent this? I couldn't come up with a reasonable response, namely, because there wasn't one. If I had it to do all over again, I'd do the same thing. The penal system has always been in my blood. At least for twenty years it was.

Nothing on the radio sounded good. It was one sullen news report after another about the tragedy in Pasadena. That's all that was on every station. I didn't need any more distraction with all the chattering already going on in my head and turned it off. Other than the wind whipping along the side of the car, the silence was golden.

I had reminisced back to the days when I first started as a correctional officer. It seemed like such a different life back then. At the time, my father was Warden at Folsom State Prison. It turned out that would be his last prison duty before retiring. I'm glad he can't see me now. Tears welled in my eyes.

A sign up ahead told me I was nearing Stockton. That's where Irene lived, where we lived. Only for me there would be no going home. Not for a while yet, if ever. Since the tragedy I've been playing it all by ear, no plans no nothing. This is so unlike me. Everything I've done throughout my entire life revolved around a carefully, well thought-out plan. Now the only option I have in my immediate future is making it to Irene's house in one piece. That's one hell of a plan.

I slowed as I pulled up toward her house and scanned the neighborhood. From a distance, I could see that something was amiss. The garage door was left open which seemed out of place. She always kept it closed. That's not a good sign. Had she been found out and taken hostage?

"The only harm that will come to her will be over my dead body," I said through hissing teeth.

As I slowly edged my way in front, I spied Irene standing inside the garage motioning for me to pull in. She'd been standing there waiting for me. What a relief. Just after I cleared the garage door, she pressed the remote. The door motored down. I made it.

For the first time in several hours, I actually felt safe. I took a deep breath. How long this will last? I don't know. Right now, it was one day at a time, make that one moment at a time.

Best thing of all, it was great seeing her again. I didn't realize how much I missed her. I slid out of the car and she fell into my arms. We held a long embrace that was long overdue, and for a short while all that previously happened disappeared. Not a word was said. I could feel her tears streaming down the side of my neck. Holding her made me realize how much we belonged together.

Finally, she moved back just a little and said, "Let's get you inside."

Wearily, I nodded. It had been a long nerve-wracking trip. My success that led to arriving up here was determined by a flip of the coin. She led the way through the garage door and into the house. It was all I could do to follow with trance-like steps.

CHAPTER 14

When I entered into the kitchen, I was overtaken with the overwhelming aroma of something cooking, and it practically knocked me down. Unless my nose was mistaken it was some kind of pasta dish. On cue, I began to salivate.

That sandwich and bag of chips I grabbed for my long trip up here were devoured hours ago. Not wanting to chance stopping along the way, I was famished.

"You'll find the bathroom just on the other side of the living room," she said.

"Okay."

Words were not coming easily for me yet. I could see that she takes great care of her house. Everything in it had its place and was so neat and clean. I know it couldn't have looked this way just for my arrival.

I felt grimy from after being out on the road all those hours today. It was a wonderful feeling washing Interstate 5 off my face and hands. If all goes well, I won't be looking at it again for a while.

When I returned to the kitchen, dinner was sitting on the dining room table. My nose did not deceive me. Irene had prepared and served meatballs and spaghetti with a fresh tossed salad. It was one of my favorite dishes.

It reminded me of a 'meatballs and spaghetti' song I sang when I was a kid. I'll put that off for another time. I wasn't feeling especially musical at the moment. It looked like a meal fit for a king. I took my usual seat.

Exiting the kitchen her eyes were locked upon mine while carrying two bottles of beer. She must be a mind reader. It was like being in the company of an angel. My eyes became moist.

"I don't know what to say Irene. If you hadn't…"

She butted in. "Save it. You haven't tried my cooking yet. You don't know what you're in for. You may want to get back in your car before you're done."

We laughed in synchrony. A heavy weight crushing my chest had been gracefully lifted off. What's more, the meal was excellent. The company was far better.

It had been one hell of a day. My mind was in a whirl. I didn't know where to begin or what to do.

Irene was watching me attentively. I cleared my throat and said, "Now that I'm beginning to recover some of my senses, let me fill you in with the real story."

She nodded her interest. "If you're up to it right now Jack."

"It would be good for me to let some of this out."

She suggested, "Okay, but before you begin let's go into the living room. I'll meet you there."

I took a seat in one of the chairs that I usually occupy. The sound of dinner plates could be heard moving about the counter. Seconds later she arrived. She pulled over one of the other chairs close to where I was sitting and faced me directly. Just after she sat, I raised my glass of beer and said, "To whatever."

She quickly came back with, "To us." We smiled in unison.

I asked, "How much have you learned from the media?"

"I imagine the same as everybody else. All of the droids murdered the inmates in the early morning hours. The cells are no longer holding them prisoner. They're defiantly not letting anyone into the prison whether they are authorized or not. It was even reported that they've armed themselves."

"What, this is news to me. I suppose had I not turned off the radio on my way up here I'd be more informed."

"You've spent the last eight hours fighting your way up here on the road. This is all new news Jack. Don't be too hard on yourself."

After a moment's thought, I blurted out, "Armed, that's impossible. There are no weapons inside the main prison."

Then it all came thundering back to me. "Shit! I forgot about the underground armory. Of course, they would have the code to enter there. They have codes for everything. But why would they take these matters into their own hands? Somebody's got to be behind this."

I sat for a moment staring off in the distance then said, "It looks like I'm going to have to back up a little. I left the prison yesterday in good standing. Nothing out of the ordinary had occurred. It was just another day at the office." I took a sip of beer.

"I arrived this morning at my usual time 8 a.m. Breakfast was just about to get underway. I activated the monitors for the cafeteria as I always do. Did. To my surprise it was empty. I rechecked the time just to be sure. There wasn't a droid in sight."

After a long breath I continued, "Right away I knew something was terribly wrong. Droids don't make mistakes or forget schedules. I continued to monitor the screens for another five minutes. Nothing had changed.

I switched over to cell one. The inmate was still in his bunk. He wasn't moving. That was unusual. They're always up by this time. I began to scan other cells to find the same scenario repeated over and over until I came to a cell where the inmate was lying motionless, face down on the floor. I initiated the cardiac monitor and brain function analysis for the cell. The inmate did not have a pulse nor register any brain activity. He was dead."

I shook my head. "I set the medical screening to automatic and performed the same tests with all the other cells. Not a single inmate showed any signs of life. They were all dead. I was beside myself. The only way this could have happened would have been at the hands of the droids. There's no other possible explanation. But the big question I asked myself was *why*? I was at a loss for words."

Irene stood and took my empty bottle into the kitchen. She returned with a full one. After placing it on a table next to me she took her seat.

I resumed, "To proceed any further was far above my responsibility as warden. Within minutes my first call went up to Sacramento; all lines were busy. On a routine basis they monitor my prison round-the-clock. That is, former prison. They had to have known what had happened. My guess would be that they were too stunned to react. I know that I was."

It was just then I remembered that one of the psychologists that took me through the facility in Sacramento had given me her card. On the back of it she wrote her cell number. She was the first one I called. She picked up just after the first ring.

"This is Valerie," her voice sounded shaky.

"Valerie this is Warden Jack Toback. We met about six months ago when I was up there for a training gig."

"Of course, I remember."

"Can you or anyone else up there explain to me what's going on? I can't get through anywhere. Every single line takes me directly to voice mail."

Without another word she blurted out, "Jack, tell me, where are you right now?"

"The same place I'm always at every morning, Droid 1."

Seeming extremely anxious she said loudly, "I'm not supposed to say this, but someone owes you this. Your life may be in serious danger. You need to get out of there as soon as possible. There's nothing further you can do. I'm not even sure what we can do from up here.

All we know is that at exactly 5 a.m. the droids followed instructions to murder all of the inmates. We don't know where or by what means those instructions got into the supercomputer, but we do know for sure that it came somewhere from the outside. So, technically speaking, you're off the hook. Your name will be vindicated soon. Just hang in there."

I pleaded, "So until that happens do you have any ideas about what I should do?"

She answered, "All the media outlets and all of the sympathizers that were against this project from the start were notified exactly when it happened. It was a well-coordinated attack all around. We know that much. It's going to hit the fan very soon, and you don't want to be around when it does."

"So that's how it is, I'm just being thrown under the bus!"

"Jack, we've all been thrown under the bus. I'm sorry. I've got to go. You can't imagine how much of a madhouse it is up here. I'll be in touch if anything significant comes about. Until then, stay safe. Get out of there now."

Before I could continue the call ended. Right then and there I knew I was on my own."

I said to Irene, "That was how it all went down." As long as I live, today would be a day I will never forget.

"We will never forget," she added.

Irene glanced at the time and said that the news at the top of the hour was just about to start. I nodded my approval and she turned on the television. It got our immediate attention.

The media was very good at doing what they always did best, showing mass hysteria. The scene shifted from the prison to a suburban area. It only took me a moment to realize I was looking at my condo from the street outside. The reporter said, "The search continues for the fugitive warden of Droid 1."

"Now they're labeling me a fugitive?" I hissed.

"They're not entirely wrong. For all intents and purposes, I had to make a run for my life. If that makes me a fugitive then so be it."

"The main thing is you're safe," Irene retorted.

"It looked like it was a smart move that I left when I did."

There was no response from Irene as we both stared at the images on the screen.

The camera showed that the front door to my door had been smashed open. It looked like someone had taken a sledgehammer to it.

The camera returned to the reporter. "We've been advised that an APB has been put out for the whereabouts of Warden Toback. At the present time we're told that he is a person of interest."

In my book that made me a wanted man.

I remarked, "Aren't they getting a little ahead of themselves?"

All Irene could say was, "I can't believe any of this is happening! It's like living through a nightmare," she dabbed at her eyes.

The scene switched back to the reporter at the prison. We could see that he was standing outside the fenced perimeter.

The reported said, "There appears to be a few hundred law enforcement personnel in addition to a military command setting up post. We heard that more reinforcements were on the way." He ended by saying that they'd been at the scene since 9 a.m.

I uttered, "That was just a little while after I had left. Even at that early on, I could already see how things were beginning to slide downhill. It was just after I arrived home that I received your call. It looks like I didn't leave a minute too soon. From the looks of my condo door the outcome might not have been favorable for me."

I looked directly at Irene and said just above a whisper, "You may have saved my life."

Her voice took on a serious tone. "You would have done the same thing for me Jack."

She's right about that. There's nothing more I could have added to that.

Irene raised her half empty beer bottle to shoulder height and held it out toward me. I picked mine up and together we clinked. No words were exchanged.

"I assume you brought some stuff other than what you're wearing," she declared.

"I packed as much as I could grab on the fly. My life is stuffed inside the trunk."

"While you're bringing it in, I've got just a few things to take care of." She stood and made toward the kitchen.

That was my cue to get what was left of my world from the trunk. On my way to the car I was beginning to feel just a slight shimmer of hope. I suppose that's the optimist in me. The three beers had something to do with that as well I'm sure.

The trunk was packed in such haste that there wasn't a spare inch of room in it. When I hit the remote for the trunk it sprung open like a jack-in-the-box. It was good for a laugh. I shook my head thinking, nice packing job Jack.

This sudden direction wasn't exactly how I planned our relationship to go. It certainly didn't include me bringing in all my personal items into her house in what was one of our first get-togethers in quite a while. It almost felt like I had the word intruder written across my forehead. Though she was right about one thing, I would have done the same for her.

When I finally lugged the last piece into the house, Irene proclaimed, "Nobody likes living out of a suitcase for any length of time. You'll find some empty closet space in my bedroom with hangers and the two of the bottom chest of drawers are empty and ready for use. Your bath towel is hanging from a hook next to the sink. An empty laundry bag is just below your towel. Um, I've got a few things to do out here. See you later." Before I could respond she disappeared out of view.

A nice refreshing shower was just what I needed to cleanse myself of what had been one of the longest and most harrowing days of my life. The hot water felt so good I almost wanted to stay in there for the remainder of the night. I dried and changed into some fresh clothes. I came out of the bathroom a new man, well, maybe slightly used.

CHAPTER 15

When I entered the dining room Irene was nowhere to be found until I heard some familiar noises coming from the kitchen. Everything had been picked up, washed, dried and put away. She was certainly a no-nonsense woman, something else I admired about her. The TV was still on. The news coverage droned on about the disaster. I'd expect it would for weeks to come. No other news of any interest seemed to exist in the world.

Nothing could surprise me at this time. A picture of me flashed on the screen with a caption under it saying, PERSON OF INTEREST. Did that mean my criminal status had been downgraded from no longer being on an APB? It most likely depended on who was reporting the news.

There's been a saying about the media that's endured centuries: *if it bleeds it leads*. I was sure that they were going to milk this story for as long as they could.

Irene came out of the kitchen and found me sitting at the same spot. She extended her hand that held a bottle of beer and placed it on the table next to me and said, "I'm headed for the shower. Make yourself at home." she turned and left the room.

I said, "Okay I'll see you when you come out." Not knowing it at the time, those would be the last words I would speak to her tonight.

When I opened my eyes, I found there was some light seeping through the blinds. It was daylight and soon realized that I must have fallen asleep. I was on the couch covered with a blanket and a pillow had been placed under my head. I must have gone out like a light!

I didn't know where my phone was so I couldn't tell the time. Oh, that's right, I took my phone apart before leaving Pasadena. I slowly sat up. Everything was still working normally.

From behind a voice rang out, "Good morning sleepyhead."

Irene came in the living room and sat down next to me. She put her arm around my shoulder and pulled me in slowly for a long tender kiss.

I hoped that I didn't have a combination of both morning and beer breath to greet her.

She smelled wonderful and said with a devilish smile, "Can you only imagine what you missed last night for falling asleep?"

She must have sensed my awkwardness and added, "Just teasing you Jack, lighten up."

After a short pause she announced, "Coffee's ready. How do you like your eggs?"

From my foggy brain came the words, "Even though I don't know what time it is I'm guessing that you probably have to be at work sometime soon."

"Not today sweetie. I called in sick yesterday. Who knows, I might be sick tomorrow too," she said with a grin.

"I've got a load of sick days coming to me, not to worry. Oh, and by the way, I got you a burner phone yesterday afternoon while you were on your way. For the time being the only person who will have your number will be me. So, you better watch out," she flashed an impish smile.

I thought to myself, 'is there anything this woman isn't capable of doing?'

I was into day two of being on the run. I felt that eventually I would be exonerated from all of the accused misdoings that had been directed at me. I knew my association with Droid 1 would forever remain a hot potato anywhere within in the penal system be it in California or anywhere else.

My time had been cooked. If nothing else, timing was on my side. I just had gotten in my twenty years. Officially, I could retire anytime now on a full pension. So, I suppose that my current situation wasn't all that bad.

I didn't know that at the tender age of forty-three if I was quite ready for retirement. I'm already familiar with the dress code: work pants with sneakers and white socks. I'd have plenty of time to give that some consideration.

Irene came into the room and said, "You look lost in thought. What's going on?"

"I was just taking inventory of my new life."

"I see, would you care to share," she asked.

I told her what I'd just been going through in my head.

"Hmm, doesn't sound bad to me. You'll have your full pension while you consider options for a fresh start."

I nodded in agreement, "You know, you're absolutely right. Things could be a whole lot worse."

We focused our attention back to the news. The situation in the south had gotten critical. According to the latest reports, it was learned that the droids would not stand down. No one was being allowed entrance into the prison.

I offered, "This might be the result of another set of instructions that had been issued from the hacker. You know if I'm thinking that then so are the computer heads in Sacramento."

I added, "I've seen what those droids are capable of doing up close. There'd be no overpowering them in hand-to-hand combat. They are just too smart, too strong, too fast and simply just too plain good.

To their advantage, the prison had been fortified to not only keep people in but also keep others out. If it came down to an all-out conflict, I wouldn't want to think about the potential casualties." A quiet hushed the room.

Irene provided sandwiches and chips for us as we continued to watch the news unfold. If nothing else I knew that there was a silver lining in the dark clouds. The tragedy of the last couple of days had brought us closer together. For that alone I'm thankful.

With 4,000 bodies undergoing decomposition and entry into the prison blocked, our country was caught in an embarrassing standoff. The White House had taken this incident seriously and it was felt that they needed to take action fast.

At the end of an emergency closed session of congress, the president declared on national TV, "My dear fellow Americans, in regard to the tragedy at the prison near Pasadena, it is the opinion of this office that risking American lives to recover the bodies would not be an option for putting an end to this debacle. We've concluded that this standoff needs to come to an end now. After a brief meeting with the Secretary of Defense and top military leaders, it's been decided that an air strike would be the quickest and most effective way to put an end to this sorrowful tragedy. God bless America." The broadcast ended.

This would be the fastest act of retaliation in our nation's history since the bombing of Pearl Harbor. It was announced that a laser-guided bunker buster bomb of unprecedented power would be used to decimate the facility. There'd be no nuclear fallout. It would leave a crater estimated to be ½ mile in diameter. Everything would be vaporized. Not a blade of grass would remain.

With the threat of over 4,000 rogue humanoids with exceptional intelligence and supernatural physical capabilities there was no other choice. Most importantly, there'd be no lives lost, at least not directly. There's always the risk of collateral damage with any type of military action. The site itself would be turned into a memorial.

Civil defense measures kicked into high gear and were reportedly now in place. Spectators and news crews were being asked to pack up any of their belongings and leave the site. All necessary precautions had started to get underway.

It was made known to the public that at 4 p.m. tomorrow, the annihilation would take place. Anyone living within a 5-mile radius would be strongly advised to evacuate any outdoor area and remain indoors.

Residents of Pasadena were being warned not to be out in the street at the time of the blast tomorrow. It would be raining life-threatening debris.

Throughout the immediate area there were emergency alerts on all TV stations and radios. Hundreds of civil defense volunteers went knocking door-to-door. If no one was home a flyer was left.

Every measure was taken to see that everyone was warned of the impending action soon to happen. Every phone number had been called. If no one answered a message was left. There were no stones left unturned.

Many volunteers patrolled the streets with loudspeakers attached to their vehicles blaring loudly the time left before the devastating blast was to occur. Everything that could be done had been done.

Irene and I remained glued to the TV along with the rest of the world for the impending countdown to destruction. All the news channels reported only on this. The detonation would be televised for all to see. It was said that more people around the world would witness this event than anything ever before in history.

In many schools, students were gathered in auditoriums to witness a sad part of history in the making. I had my reservations about that. This might prove to be the greatest disaster of the twenty-third century. I would only hope so and wouldn't want to see anything related to this disaster ever repeated.

The next day at 12 p.m., a Bishop, Priest, Rabbi, Buddhist monk and Imam were taken to the site of the prison. Each gave their blessings to the deceased inside. The armed droids did not make their presence known. It was hoped that this final act might provide closure for some of the families.

The religious ceremony was completed at 2 p.m. Without further ado they were quickly ushered off the site to an area that would provide protection many miles away.

The bomber was making its approach to the site. Fifteen-minute warnings were sounded from air raid sirens all throughout Pasadena. In this case, low technology still proved to be the best tactic for warning of disasters to come. People that had waited to the last minute quickly scurried for cover.

The aircraft wanted as much distance between the detonation and itself and maintained a cruising altitude of 30,000 feet. Now reported just 10 miles away, the weapons bay opened. Inside perched the largest conventional bomb ever to be employed for the first time on a real target. It was so big that the huge bomber could only carry this one laser-guided explosive device.

At two minutes before the designated time the president confirmed authorization of the missile launch. It was now officially a go. The bomb was now locked on to its intended target sitting just six miles below.

There was a countdown broadcast for all to hear. It was echoed by billions around the world. When the countdown finished, it announced - missile away. Thirty seconds later the earth shook violently.

To the folks in Pasadena, it felt like a massive earthquake. Many buildings suffered irreparable damage. A minute later it began to rain injurious debris. It looked like the sky was falling.

It was a clear day. The camera on the bomber showed a large impact crater where the prison once stood. A large dark cloud hovered above, slowly spreading out. Homes and structures within a 2-mile radius of the blast were devastated.

Five miles away Pasadena wasn't getting off much easier. Many homes and buildings showed significant damage. No doubt, clean-up and restoration were going to be an expensive proposition.

Just like that it was done. Droid 1 no longer existed. In one fell swoop every trace of it had been wiped off the face of the earth. Despite the years of research and funds that went in to building this project, it was one of the most senseless tragedies ever to occur in American history.

I was mesmerized by the video of the crater which now occupies the soil upon which Droid 1 was built.

I remarked, "Irene, to think just a few days ago I was standing right inside there." I shook my head in reverence.

Irene looked at me and after a long pause said, "You know, changing subjects, I've been thinking about getting a dog for a while now. I've considered a lot of breeds and have decided on a boxer. Can you offer an opinion on that? I could sure use having someone around that knows about this breed."

She knows that I grew up with a boxer from when I was just a tyke. I must have smiled from ear to ear, a woman after my own heart.

"Oh, there's one more thing. I don't know if you remember or not but you never finished your story the night we went to Sal's. It was just before you left. I think it's long overdue. I remember exactly where you left off. And what better place to resume than the first time we go fishing. And I know just the place." That will be our silver lining.

CHAPTER 16

Two weeks had gone by and I felt that it was safe to return home. I didn't want to overstay my welcome. There'd be plenty of time for that in the future. Other than being in need of a little clean up and some TLC, it was just the way I had left it. News of the catastrophe had begun to simmer down.

The following morning at 9 a.m. my doorbell rang. I wasn't expecting any company and quietly padded over to the door and peered through the peephole. I caught sight of a man dressed in a suit standing at my front door. There seemed nothing threatening about him, no bulges within his jacket that I could see.

After opening the door, I asked, "What can I do for you?"

He asked, "Are you Jack Toback?" I thought that was an odd question given that he was standing right in my doorway.

Not wanting to drag this on I declared, "Yes I am".

As he reached into his jacket, I was ready to slam the door. In his hand he held an envelope that he presented to me with an extended arm. Out of reflex I grabbed it.

He curtly said, "You've been served," then turned and walked away.

After closing the door, I brought the letter into the kitchen where my lukewarm cup of coffee awaited.

Opening the letter, I found that I had been subpoenaed to appear as a witness before the Supreme Court in Washington DC next week.

It stated that I would serve as a witness for the defense for the case of California and the United States vs. the People, a class action lawsuit. After reading more particulars within the letter, I placed it down and gave Irene a call at work. After she picked up on the third ring, I filled her in on everything.

"I had a feeling this would be coming," she said. "It was inevitable."

"I'll let you get back to work," I replied. "We'll talk about this more this evening."

While pouring myself a fresh cup of coffee the phone rang. It's been a busy morning. Is this what retirement is supposed to be like? I didn't recognize the caller ID.

"Hello."

"Hi Jack this is Governor Ryan. I'm aware that you are in possession of a subpoena to report for court next week in DC. I'm calling to let you know not to panic. We're behind you on this."

This is the first time I've spoken to the governor since the tragedy at Droid 1.

"What's going on?" I inquired.

He cleared his voice and said, "First thing that I want you to know is that all travel, lodging, food and miscellaneous expenses for your time away will be picked up with state funding. You will not spend one penny out-of-pocket. Let's be clear on that."

After digesting what the governor just told me I replied, "I can understand this case being kicked up to the Supreme Court but I'm surprised that it's being heard so soon."

He retorted, "This case presents an urgent matter before the United States and subsequently was able to get the docket cleared by the Chief Justice. The class action lawsuit damages are approaching one trillion dollars. We're talking big money here.

Your expert testimony before the court is of paramount importance to the United States and subsequently California.

You'll be met by representatives from my office and taken by private jet to the East Coast next week. Not to worry. We've got you covered. Do you have any questions at this time?"

"Probably a million," I said, "but I've got enough information to carry me forward for right now."

"I'll keep in touch," he replied and disconnected the call.

That certainly put a damper on the week. From that time forward, it just dragged on.

I received a text on Friday informing me that I would be picked up promptly at 9 a.m. on Monday morning for my trip to Washington DC. Proceedings were cleared to begin on Tuesday. This was the main topic of conversation that Irene and I shared through the entire week. We spent every evening together.

I was packed and ready to go before my scheduled pickup on Monday morning. Halfway through my second cup of coffee the doorbell rang. Two guys dressed in suits greeted me at the door.

"Be right back," I said. After rinsing my coffee cup, I grabbed my suitcase and was out the door. A limousine was awaiting me. It looked like no expenses were being spared.

When we arrived at the airport one of the guys handed me an envelope and wished me a pleasant flight. Upon entering the plane, I saw that I was the only one on board other than the flight crew. It felt kind of weird. We were cleared for takeoff and I buckled up.

Once we reached cruising altitude breakfast was served. While eating, I remembered the envelope I was handed from one of the guys in the limousine and pulled it out of my jacket. Inside was a credit card that was in my name. There was nothing else in there, not a note, nothing. The governor proved to be a man of his word.

Six hours later we landed at Dulles International Airport. It was a smooth flight. As I exited the gate in the terminal, I was approached by someone who identified himself as a federal employee. He took my suitcase and escorted me to a waiting vehicle.

After a short trip we arrived at the Four Seasons Hotel in Washington DC. At the reservation desk I found that my room had already been reserved, and I had been handed a key card. After dropping my suitcase off in my room, not wanting to explore the city, I opted for dinner at the hotel. Shortly after, I returned to my room and gave Irene a call. "All's well in DC. I miss you already," I said.

"Same here sweetheart," she replied. After a few more minutes of chit-chat we said our goodbyes.

In the morning, transportation to the courthouse had been arranged and was awaiting my arrival at the curb. An appointed attorney would accompany me.

Upon arrival, I was in awe at the size and magnificence of the building. It was quite a sight.

The attorney escorted me to a courtroom and we found our seats. While waiting for the judges to make their appearance, he went over some of the courtroom procedures with me. A few minutes later, we stood as the judges entered and took their seats. Court was now in session.

Throughout the morning session witnesses had been called to testify. Two of them I immediately recognized. They were Valerie Martinez and Director Hillsdale from my seminar training in Sacramento. Many others were paraded before the court.

The morning proceedings moved along quickly. We adjourned for lunch. There was a wonderful restaurant just down the street from the courthouse. My state sponsored credit card had been put to good use.

When Court resumed in the afternoon session, I was the first witness called to testify. My nerves were frazzled.

My attorney whispered in my ear, "They saved the most important for last."

Hearing that did not provide me with any comfort. After being sworn in I was approached by the defense.

The first question I was asked was, "Would you kindly state your name for the record?"

I cleared my throat, "Jack Toback."

It was followed up with, "Please Mr. Toback would you kindly tell the court how long you had served as warden at Droid 1."

I answered, "A little over six months." My palms were sweaty.

"Thank you."

He then said in a tone that suggested finality, "I want you to consider this next question very carefully. Mr. Toback, can you tell the court that at any time during your six plus months at Droid 1 did you ever feel intimidated or threatened by any of the droids?"

I answered without hesitation, "No, not a single time."

He then followed up with, "In your experience at Droid 1 did you ever see or hear or witness any of the inmates intimidated or hurt by any of the droids prior to the incident?"

I answered, "No. That never happened."

He turned and faced the panel of judges and said, "No further questions."

The Chief Justice asked, "Does the prosecution wish to question the witness?" Council replied, "We have no further questions your honor."

That was quick. My time as witness was done for today. But I would need to be present in court tomorrow in case I was called again to testify.

The next morning court resumed after the nine judges were seated. The Chief Justice announced, "Ladies and gentlemen and officers of the Court, we have reached a decision."

A hush spread throughout the courtroom. "In the case of the People vs. the state of California and the United States, we do not find any liability or negligence on the part of California or the federal government.

We conclude that the offenses taken against those incarcerated were from terrorists of unknown origin. It is the ruling of this court that we find in favor of the defense. This case has been dismissed."

The news from the trial hit the media in a matter of seconds, but as far as I was concerned, it was time to go home. An afternoon return flight on the private jet had already been arranged. My part was done.

It was early evening when I finally arrived home. It had been a long day. Irene had come over with a basket of food and a bottle of wine. We spent the evening catching up on all events that took place in DC. We toasted the evening. She spent the night.

Next morning Irene had to leave early for work. There'd be no time for coffee.

Just after I had finished some eggs and toast the phone rang. Caller ID displayed it was from the governor's office.

I answered, "This is Jack."

"Jack you did great," a voice rang out. It was the governor.

"Thank you, sir," I replied.

I've got something urgent I need to talk with you about. If I send someone over to pick you up can you meet me for lunch?"

Who am I to say no to lunch with the governor? "It would be my pleasure sir," I replied.

"Great. They'll be someone to pick you up at 11:00. See you later."

The governor's limousine pulled up in front of my condo at 11 a.m. Just before noon we were in Sacramento. A few minutes later we arrived at the remodeled Governor's Mansion, an historic site. Someone greeted me at the limo and brought me into the main dining room.

"Jack," I heard a voice from the side. The governor was wearing a huge grin as he embraced me in a bear hug. I wasn't quite expecting that. After taking our seats, I chose some items from a menu placed in front of me. I knew he wanted something from me. It's not like we do this all the time.

"Jack, I'll tell you why you're here. The ruling from the Supreme Court exonerated all of us from the wrongdoing that took place. In a sense, we have a clean slate." He took a sip of wine.

"I've spoken with the manufacturer of the droids and they have a new and improved generation that's ready to roll any time now. What happened before would not ever happen again. That's guaranteed, but most importantly, the public needs to know."

My antenna went up.

He went on, "The only small hurdle that stands in front of us at present is public awareness and acceptance of the new droids. In time we'll be able to bridge that gap. That's where you come in and that's the reason why you're here. We need someone who on behalf of the penal system can speak to the general public at different venues about the safety and the benefits of droids working side by side with us in society, not just the penal system. The most qualified and recognized person for this position is you."

I almost choked. "Excuse me Mr. Governor but I have no experience in public speaking. Most of my adult life has been spent in prisons."

"I'm well aware of that Jack. We're not looking for some actor. We need an honest, reliable spokesman. Someone the public will trust. You fit that bill perfectly."

I didn't have a response at the tip of my tongue yet.

"You'll be traveling around the state with a salary that will be greater than what you were receiving as warden. You should know that this position will make a great contribution to the penal system. Your father may he rest in peace would be proud."

"He probably would be," I replied in a low voice.

It sounded all too good to be true. I always wanted to be part of the generation that made major changes to the system. How could I say no?

Curiously, I asked, "What do I need to do to get this started?"

The governor extended his hand to me from across the table and said with a smile, "Just shake my hand." There was no reason in the world to give it any further consideration. I raised my hand and took his in mine and we shook. Placing his other hand on mine, He grinned and said, "Welcome back Jack."